SIMPLE
GIFTS

Also by Joanne Greenberg

SIMPLE GIFTS

JOANNE GREENBERG

HENRY HOLT AND COMPANY/NEW YORK

Copyright © 1986 by Joanne Greenberg
All rights reserved, including the right to reproduce
this book or portions thereof in any form.
Published by Henry Holt and Company, Inc.,
521 Fifth Avenue, New York, New York 10175.
Published simultaneously in Canada.

Library of Congress Cataloging in Publication Data
Greenberg, Joanne.
Simple gifts.
I. Title.
PS3557.R3784S56   1986   813'.54   86–323

ISBN: 0-8050-0034-8

First Edition

Designed by Jeffrey L. Ward
Printed in the United States of America
1 3 5 7 9 10 8 6 4 2

ISBN 0-8050-0034-8

To Sidney and Anita

Not only goodness,
but wisdom also

*Hope is a beautiful thing;
it's the waiting that spoils it.*

—Jewish aphorism

Contents

1

Kate

To get here you have to ford two creeks and go half-way up a mountain. We're in one of the rising valleys on the east leg of Croom Mountain, and the road is so rutted he said he had to stop twice. He said he kept hearing the oil pan hit rock as he ground and bucked in the ruts. It was July when he came. The sun was almost smoking with the resins baked out of the sage and thistle. The colors of our mountain are gray-green and blue-green, because even with springtime snowmelt it's so dry here in summer that the crickets seem to pop with baking at the roadsides and in the fields. He said that when he came over the last rise, he looked up and there was our place: barn, corral, house, standing in a line at the far end of the sown field. He said he was struck by their "perfect authenticity." He used those words the first time he saw us. Later we would be very busy with those words, but when we first heard them, we were only amazed.

He came out of the noon drone heat, laying a ten-mile-an-hour dust plume behind him. I was in the kitchen, working slow in the heat. Louise came in and told us there was someone. We didn't think of the postcard from the government. Now and then people come; some are only lost. Because we have no phone, we have more surprises than other people. You look up and there's someone. I like surprises, but a phone is the thing I'd get first if there were money for something new.

I went and told Mama, who was lying on the dining-room floor, trying to stay cool. Mama got up and we both went out to see who it was.

You can tell when someone hasn't been here before. There's a hesitation about where we might be; the road goes to the barn and there's a crisscross of trails through the weeds that makes the choice of house or corral. He didn't know where to stop and get out, and by that we knew he was a stranger.

So he got all the women in the family standing on the porch watching him: Jane with her paints, Louise who had been reading or dreaming on the shady side of the porch, and Mama and me, who had been in the house. We all stood and watched while he got out and came over. He had a briefcase. Salesman, we all said to ourselves, that or the government, and then we gave a sigh. It's hard to get up interest in all the things you can't afford to buy or in laws you can't afford to keep.

He looked to be about thirty years old and he was very clean and good-looking even in the heat. He said he was with something called SCELP—Social, Cultural, something, something—and I remembered the postcard, then, which Mama had stuck in the drawer with the things that had no other place to go. I said I'd go get the card, but he said it was okay because he was here and wanted to introduce himself. Then he did an amazing thing. He shook Mama's hand and introduced himself to her and then to each of us, saying Ralph Kelvin and asking us our names, Mama and me and then Louise and then even Jane. I don't think Jane ever had a grown-up ask for her name and tell her his and shake hands. It made Jane fall in love. Jane is six, and at that age most things go slow, but love can come in a minute. I'm fifteen, but I can still remember that.

Mama was taken, too. You could tell. Mama is pretty big and she likes bright colors in her clothes. With her size she looks very bright when she walks. She gave Mr. Kelvin her special smile and she told Louise to come inside to help her get something cool for him to drink. I told Jane to take Mr. Kelvin to the barn where Daddy was, and that I would go for Robert Luther, who was up at the pasture watering ring. Jane took hold of Mr. Kelvin's hand to lead him and I saw him swallow a little. Then I remembered that Jane had been working on her paints and that her hands were probably sticky and colored with what she used most—Midnight Blue, most likely. I liked him then, too, because he hadn't pulled away or given her a look. He acted as though sticky blue was OK with him.

As I walked with them to the barn, Mr. Kelvin was talking about our place. "Look at that barn," he said; "it must be a hundred years old—wood and stone, too. Look at that beam-and-wood-shingle roof. No aluminum, no plywood anywhere. Look at that corral," he said, "split-rail and handmade in a style I've never seen except in books." He told us it was Appalachian adapted from an even older one used in Wales. "Wonderful," he said, "and the house—old, authentic—wood-lapped slab on a log-and-mortar frame. Shake roof and the apron porch. An Early American adaptation of a Breton rural style. You can see familial and cultural influences—it is an American model, all right."

No one had ever said this about our place. They called it backward, poor. A lady from the Welfare once called us marginally deprived. It all meant bad, but here was this man from the Social, Cultural, something, something, praising everything he saw, everything everyone else had always said was backward and wrong. By the time we came to the barn, three kinds of stickers had been caught in Mr. Kelvin's pant legs and stuck on his socks. You could tell they were going to itch.

We got to the barn, a relief on a day like this, and I went in for a minute to be in the dark, in the hay-smell and shade. Mr. Kelvin was talking to Jane, saying he had forgotten the smell of barns. I went farther in and waited until my red-black vision cleared to the darkness. I was going to get Achsa, our horse. Daddy was nowhere to be seen. I got scared of what I knew was going to happen. The old car he had been fixing was there, its hood up in what Louise called The Crocodile. Mr. Kelvin took a walk inside, sun-blinded, and almost tripped over Daddy, who was, I saw now, lying straight as a corpse on the floor at the other side of the car, sleeping. I was about to say something, to begin the whole story, some story to try to get Mr. Kelvin away, because Daddy asleep doesn't look like anyone else dozing off his lunch. This was sure to be a bad mark against us. Mr. Kelvin said, "Good Lord, is he hurt?" and Jane surprised me because she chirped up, "Oh, no, that's the way Daddy sleeps. It's no good trying to wake him up. Don't worry, he'll wake up by himself in a little while." She said this so easily and naturally, I thought she could pass him over it. He said, "We shouldn't just leave him like that, should we?" I said, "There's nothing here to hurt him. It's so hot today, this is probably the best place."

Jane opened her mouth and began to say, "He always gets—" and I knew she would be trying to explain Daddy's sleeps. I grabbed her by the shoulder and said, "Yes, he always gets worn out in heat like this. We'll just go back to the house." Now I couldn't go and get Robert

Luther because I had to stay and keep ahead of Jane's mouth. It's not her fault; she's only six.

But Robert Luther, who knows Daddy's sleeps by a kind of instinct and who is smartest in this way of matching sight to meaning, must have seen Mr. Kelvin's dust-up from the high pasture, because he rode up then and was waiting at the barn door. We met eyes and I said something about Mama having something cool for all of us. Robert Luther got Mr. Kelvin's nice introduction and agreed that we should all go back to the house. Jane has lost her two top teeth, and she looked up at Mr. Kelvin and smiled. Louise says that Jane's smile reminds her of a victorious prizefighter. Whatever it is, it was enough for Mr. Kelvin, that smile. He smiled back at her and I guess forgot about Daddy lying like death beside the car. Robert Luther looked at me again because I was behind Mr. Kelvin. The look said, Nice man, but what does he want? I gave a little lift of my shoulder, and then we both looked around to see that nothing was in sight that shouldn't be.

Back on the porch, Mr. Kelvin began to talk about the place again. He had seen the hayforks on the barn wall, he said, the ones left over from Grandpa's time and before. They were handmade—wood backed with metal. He had seen the old-time handmade wheelbarrow and noticed the joinery of the feed boxes against the wall. All that, while we had been looking for other things in a way we had learned without ever knowing how we had learned it. Mr. Kelvin said that the barrow and the forks and the joinery were beautiful. Robert Luther looked at him quickly to see if he was mocking us. No. Mama looked startled. All the years we'd kept so many of those old things as mementos because Daddy's granddad had made them, but we had always been a little ashamed at the eyes of outsiders; they were rough, heavy things, clumsier, harder to work than the factory-made ones of the light, new

5

metal. I couldn't even use the hayforks; they were far too heavy for a girl. The barrow was a challenge even for Robert Luther, it was so bulky. Old scythes we'd replaced with the tractor cutter; walking plows we'd replaced with the harrow blade.

"Croom Ranch," Mr. Kelvin was saying, "and the wild grass sweetening in this heat." That's when Mr. Kelvin got Louise's vote. Louise writes poetry and a word means more to her than the thing itself. In that love of words, headlong, Mama says, Louise is like Jane and like Mama, all or nothing. Mama's side of the family.

We were all waiting for Daddy. Mr. Kelvin gave Mama his card and she read it and looked at me and Robert Luther with a look that said, If this is English on here, I must be from somewhere else. Robert Luther took the card and read it and gave it to me, and I read it and passed it on down the line.

RALPH KELVIN
PLACEMENT WORKER

SOCIAL, CULTURAL, AND ETHNIC LIFE
PLACEMENT PROGRAM
Human Heritage Section
DEPARTMENT OF THE INTERIOR
UNITED STATES GOVERNMENT
DENVER OFFICE

I had no idea—no idea at all. Jane took the card from Louise and smiled at it, pretending she could read. She thought the words on anything described it in every way. She thought that card had Mr. Kelvin's life history all the way to the soul. People who can't read are like that.

Then we saw Daddy coming from the barn and we all seemed to wake up together. Mama hurried in to get the drinks, Robert Luther took the card away from Jane,

Louise got up and went to help Mama, and I got busy moving the chairs out from the dining room.

As I came out holding two of them, I looked at Daddy moving toward us and I knew I was seeing him the way you see your own family when company comes—as though you are looking through the company's eyes and not your own. He looked very thin and small to me then, and not very strong or impressive. Sometimes small men are quick and fiery. Daddy isn't one of those. There was something in him that hadn't been set or decided long ago and left him always as if he was on the edge of asking a question.

Daddy was looking at Mr. Kelvin so he didn't look out for the loose spot in the porch, and when he got on it, we all heard it sing out and Daddy jumped off of it quick. Mama was back out. You could see her wither up someway. She likes things to be nice and you can tell it hurts her when they aren't. Luckily, Mama doesn't stay hurting long. She got busy worrying about whether Louise and Jane would put the company doily on the tray.

Mr. Kelvin shook Daddy's hand, "Mr. Fleuri—" No one ever called Daddy Mr. Fleuri unless they wanted something out of him. It got Daddy on his guard. Mr. Kelvin tried to talk about cattle and crops and weather. All that did was to get Daddy more and more nervous. The girls brought out the Kool-Aid and cookies. No doily. You could see Mama ache over it. We all sat down like the kids in the principal's office when somebody's been stealing in class.

Mr. Kelvin began to talk. He told us the history of the Social, Cultural, and Ethnic Life Placement Program and why it offered so much good to so many people. He told us about the Cultural Heritage Act, and when it had been voted in. He even quoted it: "Reflecting the government's wish to preserve authentic homesteads and lifeways and the ethnic richness and diversity of the nation's people." We didn't know what to say, so he kept talking, quoting and then explaining how the government's idea—SCELP—was "implemented to bring both advisory and financial functions to those on the program of Social and Ethnic Life placements." He could see we weren't understanding it, so he tried to make it simpler. He breathed out and said, "People seek nature. They seek its peace and quiet, its space, its grandeur, but the quiet and space aren't there for them anymore. The parks are full, the trails are littered. Today, people seek experiences that involve them in ways they don't practice at home. There are theme parks—first there was Disneyland; now there are ethnic-theme parks, Roots and Corazón de mi Raza, but for some people those experiences are too artificial, not authentic, not intense enough or sufficiently engaging."

We didn't know what to say. I was getting a dim idea. Next to me I could see Robert Luther working on something. Mr. Kelvin was trying hard to explain. He thought we should understand how what he was saying applied to us. "What you have here," he said, "your work, your days—think of a man who does brain surgery all day, or who invents languages for computers, or who is a theoretical physicist—*abstractions* year after year—such a person's refreshment, renewal, might come from something direct and physical, work that engages the body as well as the mind and the products of which are specific, direct, tangible . . . ."

We understood the words—most of them anyway—but we had no idea of what the government wanted us to do. I tried to figure it all out, looking at the cricket-dancing heat that watered above the wheat field. Time hung over the field and the words moved toward me for a minute until I almost understood, and then they pulled away. No one said anything until Mama sighed and said, "I'd like to go to Disneyland someday. Yes, I'd like to see Disneyland . . . ."

8

Mr. Kelvin opened his mouth to say something, and then Daddy said, "How did you find out about us up here?"

Mr. Kelvin smiled and said, "The vet told me—John Pollin, the vet in Bascom."

We all tensed up. Not only do we owe him money, but he thinks we're behind the times on the way we run our stock. Daddy said, "Do you mean you want *us* to turn this into a dude ranch?"

Mr. Kelvin took a deep breath and said, "Let me tell you about Avondale. In Alabama, there's a plantation—black people own and run it, and black people from all over the country go there for a week or two to experience life the way their forebears did—as the slaves did in the 1800s. Of course, they're not slaves now, they're professional people mostly, but they do the real work and experience the lives of those people in the past. They pay to have this experience, to eat the food, sleep in the quarters, do field labor in cotton or cane . . ."

"And what does the government do?" Robert Luther asked.

"Well, the government helps the plantation by supporting its restoration, continuing it in its year, which is 1820, and thus providing the experience for everyone. Avondale pays for itself and brings in enough surplus to fund new placements."

"Which the government helps?"

"Yes. There's a fishing village in the Northwest, four separate Amerindian experiences, a Spanish-Mexican village here in Colorado, in Ignacio, an Eskimo hunting family—"

Daddy looked up and started to say, "*Eski—*?"

Mama raised her hand like you do in school. "What do the people do? Are they tourists?"

"No, that's the whole point. They are *visitors*, but they come to work and live the life of the placement—

9

your life in this case, as you live it, for however long they're here. They're part of the experience instead of being merely spectators. You see . . . you'd run it, of course; you'd need to tell them how to work and when, to teach them, but if it were planting time, they'd plant as you directed, calving, branding, all in its season, but done as it was done back in the 1880s, which is when this homestead dates from."

"Like it was then?"

"Like your grandparents did it. Yes."

Going back in time. We would be like the pioneers, then, like Daddy's granddaddy on this place. More than a game, like July 4—real. I had lots of questions all of a sudden, but I needed time to let the idea sink in. Mr. Kelvin was saying that to go back was to get free of the awful struggle for money over product that has made life on the ranch and farm so much harder. We would simplify, he said, live closer to everything that counted. He began to talk about it, to use our barn and old tools to picture to us how it could be. We already knew all the old ways, he said, we already had the old tools in the barn, the horse-drawn harrows we could use—still did use, didn't we, when the modern thing broke down or ran out of gas? It was easier to use modern machinery only when there was no one to help hitch up horses or walk traces, bring the wood for the woodstove or take the ashes out, wash, hang clothes in the sun—it was all right for a task to be labor-intensive, he said, if the people were there to do it and people would be here, visitors who would love doing the worst and hardest jobs. Robert Luther said that no one could compete horse-drawn against a modern machine. Mr. Kelvin kept his eyes on Robert Luther and it made me know that he was a nice man, because if he had looked away it would say something we all knew: that we hadn't competed. You could look at this place with a modern rancher's eyes: forty head,

10

when there should have been four thousand; shrinking fields, and all the buildings needing repair. We had gone back already without wanting to.

Mr. Kelvin only said, "That's where the SCELP program is different. You won't have to sell your cattle; you'll be using them in part to feed the visitors. The program will pay for visitors' other food and for their lodging and for the restoration of the buildings to stability with authenticity. The program will pay for implements and clothing. The visitors will supply the labor you need—they pay the program for their participation. The land stays productive. Best yet, people on SCELP only pay income taxes on half their land. The government allows a write-off on the rest."

Daddy didn't say anything, but all the rest of us could barely keep still for questions. Mama was worried about how much we would have to give up. Robert Luther asked about how easy it would be to teach the visitors to do the work. I wanted to know how we would get the visitors. Louise wondered about dressing and how we would all look. Jane wanted to know if my friends would still visit and if we could go to Bascom to school. Mr. Kelvin answered the questions one by one without getting impatient. He kept calling us a cultural treasure and a heritage. He said the barn and the house were the history of this area, of its ethnic strains. Every so often Daddy looked at him to make sure he wasn't trying to put something over on us or make a joke. People can be cruel; I know they can.

Then Mr. Kelvin said, "The people who will be visiting you will be very gifted people with very special jobs, usually in technical fields. You'll have the chance to stay on your own place and have interesting parts of the world come to you. SCELP usually attracts doctors, psychologists, and artistic people. Talking with people like that would be better than TV."

11

"We don't have TV," Louise said. "The set went defunct."

Mama is very proud of Louise's vocabulary. She said, "Isn't that a lovely word. Louise reads a lot."

Mr. Kelvin said he didn't notice any electric lines up here.

"Are none," Daddy said, "we have a generator."

Instead of raising his eyebrows, Mr. Kelvin smiled.

Mama had been defending us for so long, she did it all the time now. She went into a big explanation of how we had a set and how it got broken a year ago and that we had never gotten around to having it fixed. Mr. Kelvin said "Oh" and "Too bad," but I could tell he knew better. There wasn't anything around here that didn't need to be replaced or repaired. When Mama finally finished, he said it was lucky that we were without it. That way we wouldn't miss it the way so many of the other placements did. "It's the one thing most of them really miss," he said, and shook his head, "but you can get it fixed and use it when the visitors aren't here."

Then Mama did something she never did with grown-up people. She asked Mr. Kelvin if he wanted to see the house. It made Daddy look up quick to see if she meant it. Mama is proud of us and of what we've done, but she only lets in the kids from Bascom that we invite for cross-country in winter or riding in summer. Sometimes people from Bascom pay Daddy to hunt up here, but they never come into the house. We all got up. Daddy and Robert Luther said they would be back at the barn.

As we went, Mr. Kelvin kept explaining more about the SCELP, about how we would be able to say how many could come and that he wanted to give us lots of time to talk it over among us. Mama guided him around to the front of the house and showed him in in a kind of careful way. Seeing her with my stranger-is-visiting eyes, she seemed to be Mama at her worst. She had on her big red muumuu and her hair had gone all wild from her nap and had not been combed. She reminded me of a Christmas present some kid has opened and then left lying around. Mr. Kelvin got more high marks with me because he didn't seem to notice.

Mama said, "All three girls and their friends done the parlor and kitchen. They done it with the *New York Times*."

"Oh?"

"They done a real nice job this time. Dr. Celestine in Bascom gets the Sunday one and he puts it in the Grange paper drive on Thursday morning a week later, and we get it out Thursday noon and we read the magazine and books and entertainment and travel sections, and Kate papers the walls with the magazine."

Mr. Kelvin said he had heard of that art and had even read an article about it, as practiced in the rural South. He said rural South as though he were saying Rome or Paris.

We came into the parlor. The room stopped him dead. He said "Oh," as though he had been hit in the stomach. It was the color. I've seen newspaper walls, too, in books at school, and two of my classes had current-events walls. Color makes all the difference. Mama, even in red, disappeared in the blaze. The parlor has an eye-level band of portraits in color of famous celebrities doing their work—runners running; politicians arguing; scientists in their labs; the President at the White House door, welcoming. Around these are banded frames of articles and, above and below, smaller color pictures in a pattern that seems to make the walls jump out and go in, in waves. The walls move. "This is an authentic work of folk art," Mr. Kelvin said. Mama ducked her head and tried to look modest and said, "It *is* stimalatin'." Mama was smiling at Mr. Kelvin.

Louise and Jane came in and you could tell Mr. Kelvin could barely pick them out of the crowd. It was authentic, and Mr. Kelvin was very strong on things being authentic. I guess what bothered him was that it was a sophisticated New York paper, because even though he praised it, you could tell it was getting to him. He kept blinking. Mama was too happy to see his problem. She said, "If you appreciate this, you'll love the kitchen, because the *New York Times* has real good pages for food and cookin'." Mr. Kelvin nodded, and then seemed sorry he did. Mama said, "Most grown-up people ain't as appreciative as you. I started it up to get the kids to know words and what was goin' on in the world and all. They took to it right away, but most grown-up people get kind of gassy with it. They don't say it but I feel it. Wait till you see the kitchen." She spoke up so the girls could hear. "Kate and Louise selected for the kitchen."

Our kitchen is like being at a hundred banquets. "Sad as you can be, you come in here and you can't help but perk up. Cakes high as heaven," Mama said, "roast beef. See that next to the devil's food? Tripe. Never liked the stuff at all, but look at it there. Almost looks good enough to eat. Sometimes when they ain't too far-out and wild, we make 'em. Steak tartare, cheese puffs, eclairs. We made that one. Worked all day. The fillin' is nothin' else but a kind of vanilla pudding, really. They don't tell you, though, the French people."

"No," Mr. Kelvin said.

You could see it was a relief to Mr. Kelvin to leave the kitchen. We walked him through the rest of the house and you could see how old and stained most of it was, and why Mama was so refreshed by her parlor and kitchen walls. I always wanted to do my walls, but we never had the money for any of it. Sometimes I think about the rooms of my friends in Bascom—Mary Bogardus has flowered wallpaper that makes you think of a magic summer meadow.

After we showed him the house, we all came back

again and sat down on the porch, and Mr. Kelvin told us more about the SCELP. We just sat there. He talked about his years in the Park Service before this program had been started. Noise was everywhere in the parks. Not sound, noise. Competing stereo music fighting on the trails, portable TV at the campgrounds, traffic jams a blue fury on the roads and gang skirmishes by the riversides, their cycles like a hundred jackhammers: *camping.*

"I need to think about all this," Daddy said, and then, "It ain't some fly-by-night thing, is it?"

"The Cultural Heritage Act is relatively new, but it is a federal program—"

"That means like the Army and the Post Office . . ."

"I guess you could say that."

"We're gonna need to think all this out," Daddy said. The way he held his face, I didn't know if he thought Mr. Kelvin was smart and right or stupid or crazy or both.

Mr. Kelvin agreed. "Of course you'll need time. I want you to take time and if you should agree to join the program, you'll need a thorough understanding of it."

"I think it's wonderful, all those tired people," Mama said. "It would be like runnin' a rest home in a way."

Daddy shot her a look under his hat. I knew Mama approved of Mr. Kelvin because she holds cultural things very high. There are knife and stove salesmen who are richer today because they did not use *ain't* or *it don't.* "I hope you'll come back. You have real nice manners and you speak real good, too, and that's so good for the kids."

"You mean they'd *work?*" Daddy asked again, and he waved his hand out to the field and barn. "Those people? Work *here* on land that wasn't theirs, for a crop they'd never see, and stock they'd get no profit out of?"

"Yes, they would, I can assure you of that," Mr. Kelvin said.

15

"It don't seem believable." Daddy looked at the car again. "It just don't seem believable."

Mr. Kelvin got up and got ready to go, but he didn't turn from us. I guess in a kind of friendly way he was hoping to turn on the middle step. We saw him put his foot over the bad place and begin to put weight on it. If you did, there was an awful squealing sound. We all opened our mouths and I half got up, but it was too late. He came down and there was the squeal and then another louder sound, something new and something we felt as much as we heard. It was too late to identify it as the sound of rotting and splintering wood giving way. Suddenly Mr. Kelvin disappeared to the waist, and as suddenly there was a lot of dust and splinters and a busyness of mice and wood beetles in the works underneath and he was standing, or the top of him was upright anyway, sticking up out of the porch floor. Because he couldn't use his legs, he could only stand there while we tried to help. Jane began to cry. "Now he'll never come back!" and she threw her arms around him. Mama began to dust him off. Robert Luther and Daddy were trying to shout through Jane's crying. Mr. Kelvin was saying "I'm all right . . . yes, it's all right, really," and to show it, he tried to lift himself up with his hands, and when he put them beside him and put weight on them to lift, they went through so that he was like an ice skater who has broken the ice and is fighting around himself for good ice to rise on and only brings off chunk after chunk. As he lay floundering, Robert Luther came to the edge of the porch and lifted him up like a puppet, Jane and all, and put him whole on the porch's top step, where Mama and Louise and I got busy looking for blood and broken bones. He said, "I really am all right," and walked down the steps with as much dignity as he could.

Daddy said to Mama, "Do you think he'll sue?"

Louise said, "Did you hear that sound? It sounded like metal, not like wood at all."

16

I stood on the porch and looked out at the barn. What Mr. Kelvin said was true. It was beautiful. The house was beautiful, too, in a way. Could your life be blessed and you not know it? I caught Robert Luther's eye. We're very close, he and I, even though we're almost three years apart. I said, "Could what he said be true?" He said he didn't know with the little hitch of his shoulder, and there was a look on his face I couldn't interpret, something wise and far, as though he'd seen something and didn't have the words yet to say what it was.

2

Jane

I decided to draw a picture for Mr. Kelvin. Everyone else goes to school, reads, writes, draws, knows and knows and knows. It will be two whole months before I go, but Mr. Kelvin smiled at *me*, came with *me*, talked to *me*, and I am the one who should make the picture that will show us to him.

The hardest thing about a picture is the size things should have: Houses are bigger than people, stock is smaller than houses and bigger if it's a herd, barns are very big. Everything has its own size and it's hard to fit all those things together in a picture, so I got Kate to tape four sheets together into a big square and that's what I used.

Our house: the porch—not after it collapsed, or even before when it was tipping over, but the way it should have been for Mr. Kelvin. Mama is on the porch with her arms out, which she does when she is happiest or maddest and when she yells to whoever will listen, "Look at this, will you!" The sun is overhead in my picture, which I like: Half the day is over by that time, usually; you know what kind of day it's going to be. I am in this picture three times. I am over here, peeking out from under the porch, because it's my special private place under there, or at least it was before the top fell in. I'm also over where everyone is standing—Kate, Robert Luther, and Louise, because we are sisters and brother—very straight and nice like a picture you would see, and here I am all alone as you come into the picture on the barn side. That's me wearing the bridal gown and holding a big bunch of flowers out to Mr. Kelvin.

Daddy is lying in the shade of Balthazar, our biggest horse. He is sleeping there the way he does, all in a minute. Everyone else turns over, stretches, yawns, and slowly falls asleep, but Daddy is either awake or asleep, just like that.

It bothered me, not getting all three of our horses in. Achsa's face is sticking out of the barn entrance, but you can't see Nebuchadnezzar at all. Louise said she would write some notes with the picture, explaining that. Our bull, Asa, is shown in the corral, but there wasn't room for all the stock, so I showed some backs of cows in there with him and here on the hill is one cow, Dinah, with her calf as she was in May. Our stock is named out of the Bible. Daddy says everything on the ranch has to pull its weight, and the Good Book is no exception.

There are some important secrets on our place. I didn't know what to do about those. One is that we have a herd of special secret longhorns that Daddy keeps down by the creek or out summering in the highest pasture. The government doesn't know about them. Sometimes Robert Luther takes me up and over the other side of the mountain to look at them. They are small and skinny and over their heads their horns are like fences that say "Stay away."

In May, when the new calves were born, I went up to see them with Robert Luther. He told me that when I went to school I could talk about school things, parties, games, clothes, teachers, chalk and books, and the kids, but not about the longhorns or our other secrets. It bothered me a lot that I couldn't put the longhorns in the picture, because of the secret, so I made one of them be behind the barn where you can't see her, but she and her calf are there and I have her eating. There's a little line of the edge of her face sticking out from behind the barn. That's the longhorn in the picture.

Daddy and Robert Luther jack deer, and that's another secret. Behind the barn is the place we park the truck. The truck is parked over the trap door, and the trap door comes up and you go down the steps into the big root cellar under the tack room of the back of the barn where all the deer are hung after they get dressed out, which is lots of times not in the season you're supposed to. Daddy says all that deer-season business is city doings. How can they ask a man to have a license and special times to hunt on his own land? Pheasant same, quail same. In the cellar, too, is Daddy's popscull that he and Robert Luther make out in the shebang in the woods. I didn't know that was secret until last year, and I'm not supposed to go out to the shebang, although Robert Luther took me out a couple of times just to see it. The stuff they make there looks like water but it smells dangerous, like snakes sleeping. I tasted it once. Someday when I can write I will write about that because it is like no other thing. Popscull spreads over your tongue too quick—you can't stop it. It runs up your nose and into your throat and goes all up and down all the trails inside you, even your head. The taste of it is terrible, but the worst thing about it is that way it spreads. I like the things I eat or drink to do what I want them to in my mouth. I will not show our cellar or the trap door in the picture. Lucky they are behind the barn anyway.

20

Mr. Kelvin smelled especially nice. His clothes smell clothy, not sweaty or barny, or greasy, or what Mama calls "ripe." He didn't smell of what he eats.

Mr. Kelvin really liked our ranch. He acted as though he liked us, too. There is another big secret. People laugh at us in town. Back in the spring I asked Kate about it, about Mr. Atkins and some other people—the way they look at us and how they say things to Mama and Daddy. Kate got mad, but later she said that people don't understand Mama very well, because being alone a lot makes her want to be friendly, and that, too, we're from the way things used to be in Bascom before it got to be all built up and full of people who eat cows but don't raise them. Louise says it's because we're poorer than most of the new people. Mr. Kelvin said it was wonderful here, that tired people would come here like you'd go on a vacation. He liked everything we *didn't* have. People in town's mouths drop open when I say we don't have a telephone and no this and no that. I like Mr. Kelvin. A lot.

The day after he came I drew my picture. It took all morning. I had to go out two or three times to see the way the barn stood and how far it was from the house and how everything looked as it stood near or far or bigger or smaller. It seemed funny, because I have lived here all my life and should know those things. Somehow I don't, though. I expect school to take care of all that.

In the afternoon I went out in the yard. I heard Robert Luther and Kate talking. They were sitting in the shady side of the house but off the porch, because they didn't trust it. I heard their voices, soft and buzzing, and I wanted to hear what they were saying, so I went onto the good part of the porch around the corner from them and sat down and listened. They were talking about Mr. Kelvin and the things he had said about people coming here and us going to be like the old-timey people. Robert Luther said, "I think it's our only chance. We don't have enough money to mechanize and make this pay. If we don't have mechanization, we need people." Kate said, "I'm scared they won't want to do it, Mama and Daddy. It's so new and they don't like new things."

Robert Luther said, "I wonder if there's a way I could find out—I read the booklet last night—all the things he left with us. It's a big jump, going back, but we'd have to keep some things—the irrigation system for one. Maybe we could keep things that don't show. They'd have to let us keep running water in the house. The inside electricity would have to go, but we could bury the line to the water pumps and have that. Or we could get the old wind pump working again. We could wear the clothes, do plowing, planting the old way, and with the program, maybe we could save the ranch and the government would give us the money to rebuild; they said restore all the things that are falling in, rotting, weathering away . . ."

Robert Luther is very smart. Kate says so, too, so I listen hard to him. Kate said, "Can we talk to Mama?"

"You can. Find out what she thinks. Dad will hate to give up his tractor, but he won't have to sell second-rate stock anymore. Mama's the one who'll really have to give up most, her washing machine, her electric stove, all the things that make life nice for her."

"And you really think it's that important?"

"I think it means saving this place."

I knew by the way he said it that this was a big thing, very serious. I wanted to ask Robert Luther what would happen to the secrets if people were out here all the time, staying over. Mr. One Eye is the only outsider who knows about the popscull and the deer. No one knows about the longhorns. They don't know in town because sometimes Papa butchers a cull, skins it, and sells it in Bascom as a calf. I couldn't ask any of this because I was kind of hiding there myself, listening, and the other thing is that I am the youngest. Kate and Robert Luther don't think I can see or hear or think or know one thing. They love me, I know, and they're nice to me—they give me rides and Kate makes clothes for me and buys me ribbons and candy, but they never really see me as a *me*.

I can bridle the horses, for example; I can stand on a feed bin to do it. Robert Luther taught me way back last year, but he forgets he did, and Kate doesn't realize I know how. It's the same with ideas. They don't think I get any, or that I notice anything. When I asked Kate about the way people act to Mama and Daddy in town, she stared at me so long I started to cry. And she said, "How do you know that? Who told you that?" How could I tell her that nobody told me, and that it hurts when she says those things. People like Káte. She has lots of school friends, even rich town kids. Robert Luther is very quiet in town, but people respect him. They think I'm cute and they are nice to me, too, but that doesn't stop them laughing at Mama and Daddy where I can hear it. They don't think I know. Sometimes they talk about Louise, too. I heard Mrs. Mason at the post office say, "That girl has a mouth on her." I think it's about the way Louise says things sometimes. She uses big words from the books she reads, and the way she says things makes them stay in your mind a long time.

Why do they laugh at Mama's friendliness? Is it because she says out loud things people think to themselves? Mama says, "Start supper, Kate. I'm in a fashion show in Paris, France." Sometimes she uses words she reads or used to hear on TV. Once we bumped into Mrs. Bogardus at the grocery store and Mama said, "Honey, you look spectacular!" and Mrs. Bogardus just stared after her like you'd stare if you saw a longhorn loose in the streets of Bascom.

In the evening after supper we all talked about Mr. Kelvin and his plan. I was expecting Robert Luther and Kate to talk a lot because they were so serious about it when I heard them in the afternoon, but they looked at one another hard at the beginning. The look was a secret message not to say anything. Everyone else said things. Mama said she thought the SCELP was a wonderful idea. We could put in a lawn and picnic tables. We could get some Japanese lanterns and have dances in front at night. "And the house—periwinkle blue with white trim—and flower boxes in the windows with geraniums, and a hot tub, and a lawn, and a grape arbor, and visitors could walk there in the evenings and that's when we could put out the Japanese lanterns."

We all sat and looked at the table for a while and then Louise said, "Did you ever think how many grass-hoppers we have? They're like popcorn when you walk. Would tourists come to see that?"

I told them I thought Mr. Kelvin would know if people would come. Then Kate said they probably wouldn't give us money for a lawn or grape arbor, and not for a hot tub, but we'd get wood to fix the porch and the fences, and best of all there would be people to help.

Mama asked Robert Luther what he thought and Robert Luther just said, "I like the idea. I think we should try it," and Kate said, "Me, too." Louise shrugged yes.

Then Daddy said, "You all got big eyes, money eyes, grape-arbor eyes, lawn-seed eyes. But you ain't got no memories. You're new as calves. I remember the gov-ernment schemes we've had—the animal regulation scheme, the inspection scheme, the license for hunters scheme, the milk inspection scheme, the feed scheme, the land allotment scheme, and all of them to help us, protect us, raise our land's value, fix us, and be for us and benefit us!" His face got kind of red and he had already talked more than he usually did but he wasn't stopping. "First they ask you to cooperate and in six months they're suggestin' and six months later they're requestin' and six months after that it's the law and you're fined if you don't and your stock and ground is declared unacceptable. It's the same bunch promotin' this, can't you see it?" And then he breathed that long way out that tells when he's going and he slid off the chair, easy, all bone-soft the way he does and never gets hurt and he was fast asleep. So we got up and cleared the table and waited for him to wake up. Daytimes it takes about fifteen minutes, so he gets as much sleep as anybody else, I guess, but like Mama says, "arranged different." It's best not to move him. He gets mad when you move him.

We cleaned up the table and did the dishes and went out on the porch, where we walked around the broken part. We all had an idea of what we hoped would happen. All different. I wanted to see Mr. Kelvin again because he was so nice. Daddy just saw a man from the government. Mr. Kelvin has nice hands and a nice smell and nice smile. Some things it's not smart to talk about at all, even on the porch after supper with people you love.

Daddy came out when he woke up and sat down and said, "You all think this thing"—and he took Mr. Kelvin's card out of his shirt pocket where he had it—"Social and Cultural and Ethnic Life Program—I don't even know what half of that means—you all think it's gonna be a great thing around here. Well, I don't and that's that," and he flipped the card off the porch into the weeds near my hidey hole.

No use arguing. We all just sat there quiet and looked out at the night coming in and nobody said anything. When it was too dark to see and beginning to be cool enough to go in, they started moving the chairs back. I slipped down off the porch and went where I saw the card fall and picked it up and put it in my pocket, and when I could I went upstairs to the attic, to where Robert Luther had his room, and put it on his pillow.

When I go to school I will learn how to think about what happened. Because I disobeyed Daddy; I went against

25

him, in a way. Robert Luther and Kate and even Louise would think I was too young to have feelings or a vote about Mr. Kelvin's plan, but I did vote in a way that they wouldn't laugh at. The card doesn't have a little body and a high voice. The card is not a little kid who can't even read or write.

3

Dreams

Their dreams: In his day-sleeps, Akin Fleuri has no dreams, but at night, though his sleeps are short, he sleeps on his back like a dead man and his dreams are simple and brutal as stubbed toes. He dreams about fires in the barn, the light breath of first smoke detaching itself from the twining mist of a mountain dawn; of grasshoppers by the thousands, a mat of them, seething in his green wheat; of manges and spavines and abortions in his dwindling herd. Most usually, he dreams of his longhorns, the hidden unregistered herd he has inherited from generations of runaways lost in the mountain valleys of the Croom. Tonight the longhorns got out and wandered the streets of Bascom and were killed by the police with riot guns. When they all lay dead, in the deserted streets, seeming bigger in death than they had been alive, the sheriff cried, "Whose herd was this?" and Akin at last said, "Mine."

Mary Beth's dreams are patched and incongruous. In her dreams anything is possible. She can fly like a bird or swim like a fish. She has the power of all languages and the secrets of science lie at her hand. Sometimes she gives lectures or speeches at the principal universities of the world and visits with all its nobility, her muumuu gleaming with jewels as she accepts praise. Tonight she was in one of the stately homes shown in the *Times*. She was a bird flying through the house, happy that there was no kitchen or bathroom in it, no furniture to dust and keep, nothing to put away, no sign of muddy feet on the deep-pile carpets, only the breath of wind stirring the white drapes. It was a place made for poetry and looking at the lights and the shadows, not for cooking or using the toilet. Against the wall were the shadows of family, but no needs. Servants did all those things. I think I'll take a dip in the pool.

Robert Luther tears up the beds he sleeps in, thrashing, contending. He runs races and flees pursuers. Sometimes he wins these races; sometimes he loses; but the challenges are always of speed or strength, and almost always competing against men and teams stronger or more fleet than he. Tonight his stage was dark, but he moaned and thrashed all the same.

Kate dreams in color and the color is part of the dream. Once, when Mrs. Lindorn had shown slides of Watteau paintings, Kate had smiled to herself in recognition, because Watteau had dreamed in the same sad-sweet colors, colors that said, good-bye, good-bye. She dreams literal, ordinary dreams of home and school, of dances and parties, and of walking with friends in familiar places. What transforms her dreams are their colors—delicate dawns that wash her common scenes with iridescent light, blue-purple snow and shawls of white-on-white, the laughter

28

of friends all she could track of them in the winter dusk, and sometimes Billy Daner or Chuck Moore walking with her in the black-green–blue-green of spruce forests behind Croom Peak, as storm clouds blow down on their trail.

Louise lies curled around her dreams, protecting them. They are secret messages—minute mysteries in symbolic form, metaphors of deep significance, poetic or mystical. Long-robed priestesses beckon the way to hidden waterfalls; ghosts fly like bats from enchanted caves. Tonight the teacher came into the class dressed in jail clothes, a number sewn neatly on the front pocket of her uniform. She said to Louise, bitterly, "Now you've done it; now you've really done it."

Jane wanted to dream about Mr. Kelvin. She had lain straight in the bed thinking about him, hoping she would see him and be with him all night, that they would walk together hand in hand, but the dream was beyond her control and she dreamed instead of coloring with her crayons a large, involved picture and of working hard to keep within the lines. It was a worry she often had because she had not been to kindergarten, where children learn such things, and now she was frightened of going to first grade and the smart, accomplished children who would be there. When she woke, she thought that had she been Mr. Kelvin's daughter, she would have been better. He would have taken her to kindergarten and helped her to be as smart as all the others. She felt a little ashamed of this and vowed to be a better girl.

4

Kate

Summer used to be my favorite season but now I'm old enough to miss my Bascom friends. I like school and its activities. On bad winter days we stay down in Bascom and sleep over at our friends' houses. Then, we're part of their town lives, and those are nothing like ours. I go with Mary Bogardus, Callie, Cimi, Mary Anne Blanke—it's the best group in the school—the smartest, the most interesting, and the most fun. Back when we were all in grade school, I got to be part of it, to belong, even though our family is not rich and I never had the clothes and toys they had. Now it's getting harder. It's getting impossible. They all go away for the summer to camp or on vacations. They go skiing or skating. You need money for all of it and special clothes and equipment and lessons and admission fees. People get tired of paying your way just so you can go along. They like me, but they're drifting away and we all know it. When Mr. Kelvin came up and talked about how the program would work, I thought about the families—maybe even boys and girls my own age—the people he said would come.

What would summer be like then, every week or so with new, exciting people? It would be nice for a change that they had to be brought along in a way. I watch Robert Luther and see that he keeps thinking yes, yes, as he faces this and that problem. It looks like a dry summer, and that means more dependence on the pumps and wells and more damage from animals coming down to eat and a harder time for everyone. Mr. Kelvin gave us time to think; when I thought, I saw how far we were sliding. Because we're as poor now as we can be and still squeak by—I mean in school and in town.

My wanting people up here is selfish, but not only that. Visitors would be good for Jane. She'll start school in the fall, but it takes time to make friends if you don't know how. Louise never learned what to do to be popular, and I know she'd learn more if different people were here.

But I wonder how visitors would take Mama. She does spend a lot of time dreaming out loud. I used to be afraid of what she said in town, and you can't cover it up. Even Jane sees it. Mama is very kind and good, but she has funny ways of talking and thinking. Years ago when I heard people laughing, I tried to be the kind of person they wouldn't laugh at. I still hear things Bascom people say, especially the new people, and it still makes me uncomfortable and ashamed. Once I admitted that to myself, it helped a little. Maybe the visitors, if they are the smartest, best people—the kind of people Mr. Kelvin described—maybe they will understand Mama better than the Bascom people do.

Robert Luther said it was the only way short of a miracle that would save the ranch. Then Daddy said no, and for the first time I can remember, I thought that if there were a way not to listen, a way to disobey without Daddy knowing, I would. It surprised me. Daddy is not a good rancher or a good farmer; you can tell that by what the town says, and what other people say, government inspectors, vets and county agents, and other people who've come. I love him, and he's a good person, and I never had an idea to go against him until now.

The day after Daddy said no, One Eye came up. We loaded the old truck with forty gallons of Daddy's shebang product and the two deer he had gotten and hung in the cellar.

One Eye is the ugliest man I've ever seen. Mama told me that years ago he got burned in the face when he was drunk, and as soon as he could breathe without a tube in his throat he got up and left the hospital as he was. He used to scare me because one side of his face is—smooth. There's no hair on the head, no eye, no eyelashes, no ear, no lip on that side, no beard, a kind of nothing all the way down to his jaw. He has missing teeth, too, so it's hard to understand him, and he's big—six-foot-three or so, and Mama says he must weigh 250 pounds—an ugly giant, ugly even on the good side of his face, which is blotchy and hairy and has little pits in it which were pimples when he was a boy.

Louise says he must like being ugly because he does it really well. I think it's good for the kind of business he does, which is selling and buying illegal things. He sells everything the government takes off the market or doesn't allow, and he says he likes to come up here, although it's no big profit to him, to get good honest contraband. I don't like him and it's not only because he's so ugly. He always kidded me but lately he is saying sex things to me all dressed up as fun. He kids Daddy, too, but not the way they do in town. Daddy likes it; you can tell. "Why don't you sell them runty cattle of yours for goats—they ain't no bigger 'n goats."

"Yeah, and they're mean as goats."

32

"Then run 'em in races, why don't you—they sure ain't worth killin' to eat."

"My cows are so tough I'm gonna train 'em to eat meat."

"Why don't you plow under this good-for-nothin' crop of broom corn and plant somethin' that'll make us both rich—marijuana, coca leaf, opium poppy—why, with your land and my contacts we could be princes. Keep up your popscull and we'd corner the market."

"What do I want to grow that foreign stuff for. Popscull, why that's another thing. In that, I figure I'm in the lumber business. I cut trees to burn and still-out my product and I grow good American corn and good American wheat, and my popscull is made of that." Daddy's eyes would shine and he would talk and joke with One Eye in a way he never did, even with us.

I don't like One Eye but I like how he makes Daddy laugh and be happy and not be nervous about falling down asleep when he needs to. I wanted to tell Daddy that maybe if we did the SCELP other friendly people could come—people who would see Daddy the way Mr. Kelvin did, as a good man on his own land, not the way town people do. It was no use talking; we couldn't even start the subject. We loaded One Eye's truck while they stood and kidded and dickered, and I left before One Eye got to talk to me. I went up on the range and picked Orpah out of the bunch and drove her down to the corral, because of a foot infection she had.

Robert Luther came over to look at Orpah's foot. When we were bent down with me holding the foot, he said, "Look at this," and showed me the card. "Somebody put this on my pillow. I think it was Mama."

"Why?"

"I think she was telling me that this once, just this once, we've got to get our way."

"Did you ask her?"

"I can't. It would mean she'd have to come out and say she'd gone against Dad and that we should, too."

You see now why I think Robert Luther is so smart. I said, "How can we do it?" He shook his head and said he didn't know.

Later, when I was making lunch and Mama was upstairs, Louise came in. I asked her what she thought about SCELP. She said, "Mama dreams for fun, but Mr. Kelvin dreams for the government. It scares me but it's exciting, too, to be in someone else's dream."

"So which is it—do it or don't do it?"

"Do it. Something's got to change around here."

Louise surprises me when she says things like that. I forget that she's growing up, too. I asked her if she was the one who put the card on Robert Luther's pillow. She said no. It must have been Mama, then.

All that day and all the next and the next I looked at us, at the land and the buildings, and tried to see in them what Mr. Kelvin had seen. When I wasn't working, I was walking around studying the house and barn, learning how far we have come on the way to being ruined. Our stock was runty the way One Eye said, skinny and almost as wild as the longhorns. On Wednesday Robert Luther and I went to see Martin Swenson on his ranch on the other side of Bascom. We said we were going to see school friends just for one afternoon, but we really went to see their ranch.

The land there was rich and flat. They used combines and raised all their own feed—alfalfa, hay, grasses, and grains. Their stock was twice the size of ours and nothing was falling apart. Being mechanized, they didn't need wranglers or hired men, except once or twice a year, and not many then, although their herd was huge. Their family was hardworking, but no better than ours when you get down to it. All the kids were going to college, or

34

had been already. I saw how quiet Robert Luther got about that. We didn't say anything all the way back. Our eyes were full of pictures, comparing.

As the days went on, I tried to look at us with my old eyes, my ordinary eyes, from before—just the barn and the house and just us. I couldn't. Mr. Kelvin and what he said had changed me, and changed the way I saw our future. I guess I had never thought about us as having a future and I saw me growing up, finishing high school, working at a job, married—the pictures I get are so small, I only see myself in them. Mr. Kelvin had been trying to show us a picture of the whole family and Croom Ranch. It wasn't envy of Swensons or what they have that finally decided us; their ranch only made us look harder at ours and know we had to do something—and soon.

On Saturday we worked all day, but in a kind of fog. We were thinking about the Social, Cultural, and Ethnic Life Placement. At lunch everyone was quiet, even Mama, and at dinner she said, "Sometimes I hate to look around and see everything so broken down, weathering, wearing." We could tell by that, that she had been working things over in her mind, too, thinking about us and this place. "Maybe if we had some awnings—some flower boxes . . ." and her voice just sort of faded away.

Louise sat at the table with that dead-dog look of hers. Then, Jane began to cry. She didn't cry aloud—I guess you would call it a weep; there was a tear, one big tear swelling up in her eye and over and down, rolling down her cheek, big and fat. Mama looked at her and started to cry, too.

It's Mama's way. She's always been like that. She says that when a woman becomes a mother, her glands and things get attached to the baby that's inside of her.

35

I asked the phys. ed. teacher about that and she said it wasn't so, but Mama swears it is, and she always laughs when we laugh and cries when we cry. I don't think Daddy ever noticed that.

So there they sat, Jane and Mama, not making a noise, crying, and when I saw them I knew how to win this fight as surely as I ever knew anything. Daddy looked around. I could see him trying to find a way to get out of it without saying anything, but we were too strong for him—just all our faces set and water flowing at both ends of the table.

"Goddamn it! Nothin's changed!" he yelled, louder than he needed to. "What do we want with public life—strangers to please and play up to? Eighteen-eighties and us—standin' in for people who are dead and gone—us fakin' their ways—for what? The government? You want more government that's give us herd inspection and tax mess and a sea of papers to fill out every time you look around—it's only craziness—forget it!"

And even as he yelled, I saw that we all knew. I read their faces one by one, Louise last of all because she thinks easier than she feels. We didn't answer, we didn't argue, we didn't explain. We stayed where we were and picked up the new weapons. It's hard to make a war against someone you love. In my mind, I called it The War of Jane's Tear.

I'm not proud of what we did. There was a way to fight and win, but any one of us could have ended it anytime. We didn't because we all dreamed the land could be saved and the ranch changed and wonderful and ourselves made new, better, richer, most of all, safer. Suddenly, we were all like Mama, who always sees everything in a kind of dream-glow, except that this was real, possible, at hand, if only Daddy . . .

We left the table when dinner was over, taking Daddy's plate in, same as always, but there was no laughing or joking as we cleared the table. We went out on the porch after the dishes were done and sat with Daddy, but nobody said anything. We just sat still, the way you do when somebody's died. It wasn't hard to do this—we all felt sad; we just let it show. The war was to *be* sad even when we didn't feel it—to act hurt, all of us, all the time Daddy was around—I guess it was a kind of practice for acting like we were 1880s people.

He fell asleep on the porch, and as soon as he did Mama said, "You know this isn't fair." Robert Luther said, "We're gonna lose the ranch if we don't," and Mama said, "Still . . ." and that was all. I think Mama was the only one who didn't have *some* fun fighting The War of Jane's Tear.

We knew we still had two weeks—Mr. Kelvin had said when he would come up to talk more and hear our questions. We measured our time by that week, and we learned that wars do funny things to time. The days pulled out like they do in calving season, hour by hour. We were all glad to get away to work in the pastures or in the house when Daddy wasn't there, but the war hung over us the way a big school test does, a life suddenly gone long and heavy.

The War: Daddy's food was always hot and on the table when he wanted it. This was one of his big complaints, that he had to come in and then wait for his lunch or dinner. Now we had it there smoking away on the table and everything set up so perfectly there was never any need for him to ask for a single thing. His clothes were clean, underwear laid out every day and no buttons off or rips or holes. Sir-ing and ma'am-ing, which we did without once forgetting; attention, obedience, more than he could ever ask for or ever did ask for and all of it cool and sad as a stillborn calf.

He took it for a day, then two days, without mentioning anything, and then he began fighting back, but his fighting was only punching away at tears and silence and sad looks. We jumped up at his word to do every job. We pitched hay, which we all hate to do, without one complaint—without any word at all—and he turned and struggled in our war and found nothing to hold on to.

"Why are you in here now, when there's work in the barn!"

"I did the barn, sir, early this morning."

"Shoveled it out?"

"Yes, sir."

"All of it?"

"Yes, sir."

"Or did you leave the corners?"

"Louise came out with me and did the corners."

In the old days, when we did more than he had asked, we would be smiling and proud and he would question us as his way of praising us. He can't praise us outright, it isn't his way, but when we knew he had seen the joke, we were telling him we had wanted to please him. Now, the things we said were to show him Jane's tear again.

The fourth day I almost surrendered. Daddy was trying to fix the irrigation system. It works on an old pump and the water comes up all day during the season, filling the ditches we've cleared at the sides of the fields. We have wooden pieces that fit the ditches, and we put them up or take them away to make the water go here or there. Daddy's grandfather built it and Daddy changed the wind powering of it to electricity years ago. Now, they've come out with so many new things, no one has the old parts anymore. The pump is old and breaks down and parts wear out. Daddy was tightening a fitting on it and the worn thread wouldn't hold and some of the machine fell back into the well hole. Daddy began cursing, which I knew he would. He told me to go get Robert Luther, but he looked so tired this time, so *whipped,* that I nearly sat down beside him and cried. It was all I could do to say "Yes, sir," in that sad way, as though he'd done it to himself, and go on down the field. Robert Luther was working with the hay cutter in the shadow of the barn, and when I told him about what had happened, he saw how close I was to giving in. He stood up and said, "Come on back with me," so we walked back to the field. On the way he told me that this was the reason we should stay in the war—there was no money for a new system or even a new pump, and no matter how much product they made out at the shebang in the woods, and no matter how many deer they took with the lights Daddy had rigged, and no matter how many quail they took and sold out of season, we would never have the money we needed to keep the ranch going. "The cutter I'm working on is going to come apart the same way—no parts, so we have to improvise—and the thing limps along and that makes it shake and the shaking fatigues the fittings and there we are again."

"But he looks so bad—I thought he was going to break down and cry."

"I know," Robert Luther said. "I see him sitting at supper—the best time of his day—looking around at all of us, and I know it's all changed because we're doing this to him. Did you see him stirring around at his dinner last night like all the taste had gone out of it?"

"None of us ate much. I thought it was the cooking. You know how Mama gets when she's thinking about something else. She's as likely to use sugar as salt and cocoa instead of cinnamon."

"Remember those beans we had that time last fall?"

"Remember that *cake*?"

We started to laugh and recall the times Mama's cooking got absentminded. Once she confused the flour measurement with the sugar. She often forgets that she has put baking soda in something and adds it again and again. Another time she put cayenne in the beans instead of paprika, plenty of it. Every now and again, Mama gets taken with a recipe they have in the *New York Times*. While she's making it, she likes to go to the party at the fashionable home it was made at. She dreams about the table and the setting that they show, and then she turns on the radio and gets some dance music or chamber music like they might be hearing and she describes it all so well you think you're there yourself. Sometimes, during all of that, the dinner will burn or the cake will fall, because she's put cornstarch in it instead of baking powder because she wasn't looking at the boxes.

We all try to watch over Mama. We love the worlds she makes and how happy they make her—there's a funny wisdom in Mama that has to do with what's important and what isn't. When I'm cooking with her I pay attention to what she's doing while she talks and sings. I watch when she's sewing, too. Sometimes we laugh about it. That laughing heals our town pain and the pain of being poor. Robert Luther and I were doing it this time to make ourselves feel better about the war.

When we came in sight of Daddy again, we had to stop. Our laughing and joking had made us forget that we weren't a family anymore, but five versus one in The War of Jane's Tear. Daddy looked up as we came on with our faces held in that sad, cold way, and I saw the puzzlement he had with it. He said to me, "*You* didn't have to come back here—I told you to send your brother, not to bring him."

I said very respectfully and very long-faced, "Yes, sir, I'll go right away," and all the way back I had to tell myself out loud that it was for his own good, for the family, for the ranch, and the cattle, and when I was done it sounded as bad to me as it would have sounded to Daddy, had he been there listening.

Dinner was the same funeral meal it had been for four days. Mama fidgeted and couldn't say anything. I realized that this war must be hitting her harder than anyone else. She couldn't stand with us, not for long and not completely, and she couldn't take Daddy's side against us either because she loved us, too, and she must have thought we were right. She was like one of the birds that flies up from our wheat field and is beaten by the wind that's blowing the ripe grain. It wants to fly against the wind and can't and it hangs there, resisting as long as it can. Mama was looking from me to Robert Luther and from Robert Luther to me and then at Daddy. I had made sure the dinner was perfect—nothing he could complain about, nothing he could get angry at and not know he was unreasonable. I knew the happiness that generals feel when their ideas work. Back last year Robert Luther had told me about tactics and strategy when we were studying about the Civil War. This noon when I had nearly given up he had said, "Our strategy is good, and while our tactics are hard on Dad, they're not cruel. The cause is good. We should be calm inside and steady, like a doctor, not a soldier." But I saw he was unhappy, too.

On the war's eighth night, Daddy broke. It was a Sunday. Mama likes religious stations on Sunday. She listens to "Church of the Air" and "Calvary Meeting" and "Church in the Wildwood," one after the other, for the hymns and the organ music, and for the sound the sermons make. Mama is not very religious but she loves poetic words. Reverend Stanhope is her favorite. "He goes on," she says, "diddle-*um*, diddle-*um*, restful as music. Like ice skating."

I love Sunday and in summer my friends used to come up. So it was harder to be cool and sad in front of Daddy and ask him so politely if he wanted more potatoes or if he wanted his cigarettes brought to him when he sat down. Daddy's sleeps are regular even though they're not when other people sleep. On Sunday he slept three times—once after breakfast and then right at Sunday dinner, falling off the chair neat as ever, and we laid him out on the floor, and then again before supper, and that worried us all.

We got through supper and we had all finished and I started to get up and clear away, and Daddy said, "All right, damn it, you've won. You've whipped me, and I hope you enjoy the winnin' like you've enjoyed the fightin'," and he went away out the door alone. Mama and everyone was sitting at the table, still. I had the gravy bowl and the potato dish in my hands. I wanted to reach out and touch Daddy, but with both hands full I could only stand there. After a minute, looking, I went out to the kitchen and put the bowls down. The War of Jane's Tear was over and I was the one crying. To this day, I don't even know why.

So then we waited for Mr. Kelvin to come, planning what we would say, and we tried to talk Daddy into seeing how good it would all be. Robert Luther took him for a walk. They were away for an hour, just the two of them, and Robert Luther must have said a lot because when they came back Daddy seemed less angry at us and less bitter about the idea, though he said he would not dress up or wear a funny hat or turn into an actor on his own place. Mama was still talking about getting awnings and window boxes and having a grape arbor.

5

Kate

Mr. Kelvin came up again. There had been no rain for weeks and everything was yellow-dry, snap-dry. The dust of his coming hung yellow in the heat and you breathed it, furry with wild sage, like breathing the burning boilovers in an oven. I was amazed at how different he looked—how much smaller. We had all thought about him so much, seen him in our minds filling up the space between us and the outside world, that we were surprised to see him human size. It made me know that the President of the United States or a movie star looks no bigger than any other person. We got shy, seeing him, then we took a deep breath and said yes to the SCELP.

Daddy and Mama signed papers that said they wouldn't sell any of the stock or anything without permission, and we signed papers about promising to be part of the program; even Jane signed—her first signature, an X in red crayon, and her promise to wear the clothes when visitors were here and use the artifacts and practice the life-style.

Good-bye to bubble gum, comics, TV, modern toys—and here he named a whole lot of things like Barbie dolls and Cabbage Patch Kids, computer games and electronic games. Then he talked about games we could play here. Most of them we had never heard of. He used words like *labor-intensive* and *land-intensive* and Louise said it all sounded like work-intensive, and Mama shot her a look because she was afraid Mr. Kelvin would be put off by Louise and not let us get on the program.

If we started to go back now, he said, Mama could move her refrigerator to an outbuilding and use it when the visitors weren't here. Before the actual visitors came, there would be a SCELP worker or two to help see that things were going right for us. He said he would start putting in our requisitions right away so we would have what he called an Enablement to Encumber. That meant to get some money. I thought his government language was interesting. All the words sounded as though they came from describing something scientific like a chemical reaction or a body part under a microscope. He was enthusiastic and his eyes got bright as he talked about how the ranch would be self-sufficient, the way it would blossom out. Daddy didn't say anything, but Mama began to talk again about the flower boxes and the awnings and the grape arbor and a patio. Her face lit up the way it gets when she's in the warm parts of her dreams. Mama doesn't drink, but in her world, graceful people are always drifting here and there on lawns in front of mansions, while music floats out and there is always champagne. Mama has never tasted champagne, but she has described it to us many times, as it is served in long crystal goblets. She talked about a lawn party and white dresses, and we could see Mr. Kelvin was getting more and more upset. At last Mama saw it and realized that Mr. Kelvin didn't know she was dream-playing, which she always does when she is uncomfortable, so she said,

"Well, maybe not the awnings and maybe not the patio, but the flower boxes—could we have the flower boxes?"

Mr. Kelvin looked uncomfortable then, and said, "Well, if you can find a picture taken in the 1880s of a farm or ranch out here that had them, well, I guess you could get them, too."

Mama smiled. Then we all smiled.

So, we were in the SCELP program, signed up and filled out, and all of a sudden, changed. Every day we thought of and talked about new possibilities of dressing, talking, and living. We had hundreds of things to write down and questions to ask. We learned how to Request to Enable to Encumber. We spent hours with lists and mailings and sent away for sewing patterns and started to make the long dresses we would wear when the visitors came. Daddy and Robert Luther got busy ordering lumber and hardware. Mr. Kelvin said to put it on the cuff because SCELP would pay for it. We were fixing everything that was worn out and broken and building a chicken house and little run and a pigpen. Robert Luther got the old wood-burning stove out of the barn and cleaned it up, and moved Mama's electric range out onto the porch and covered it. "Oh, Lord!" she said, "don't take my refrigerator yet! Don't take my washer till the people come!" and she threw her arms around the machine. Daddy bit his lip and it made me feel like crying, because down in Bascom they don't see his character. He never said to Mama, "This is your doing; shut up and bear it," which he deserved to say, and she deserved to hear. He only said, "Kate, you watch your Mama and learn to use that woodstove," and then he went out to the barn. They were married out of high school, Mama and Daddy. How did she know to pick him out of all the rest? How did she know what was inside when he talked so seldom and never about what he thought? When the time comes, will I know how?

45

A week later we were back on kerosene for our lighting. The lamps had a sweet yellow glow but you couldn't read the small print in paperbacks with them. We decided to use kerosene in all the rooms but the dining room, where we studied and read, at least until the visitors were with us and the paperbacks were gone.

In the middle of all our changes, One Eye came up with the whiskey bottles for Daddy's popscull. Robert Luther says One Eye cheats Daddy, but there is nothing we can do, and since it's all against the law, there's nothing *anyone* can do. We were, at least Daddy was, glad to see him because we suddenly needed lots of money for things the SCELP didn't have vouchers for, or couldn't give us right away.

He came when we had the old binder-reaper out of the barn being cleaned up, and the old harnesses out, and he laughed about it to Daddy. He seemed a little restless this time. He wanted more product, he said, and why didn't we turn our time to product and quit fooling with our play-toy herd and our play-toy equipment. That part was usual for him, but this time he seemed more serious about it—almost angry. We got shy about the SCELP and didn't say anything. I wanted to tell him off—I wished Daddy and Robert Luther would; but no one did, and we loaded up the last batch of product that we had waiting in the cellar under the barn, while he and Daddy laughed and joked. I try never to be alone with One Eye. In front of other people, he says, "Here's Miss Kate lookin' like spring," then, loading product or waiting for the men to come up with a heavy deer carcass, he leans too close and says, "You'll never get a man that way, Miss Kate, with your knees all covered up and a high neck like that. You should be showin' some of them girlie goodies around a little." I want to strangle him when he says things like that. It's hard enough to be poor when your school friends aren't, to know that their clothes and trips and colleges will not be for you. It's worse to think that you may not be pretty enough even to get by in Bascom High. During the summer I knew I had changed a little, but I wasn't sure how, or if my changes would be OK with the kids in school.

It got me thinking about the way I would tell my school friends about the SCELP. Bascom is still a small town, too, even though it's gotten to be a suburb. Most people are much richer than they used to be but they still judge things in the careful way small towns have. I wondered if they would think we were Welfare people, or if the town kids whose folks worked where we bought things would think we were deadbeats, since it would take some time to get those government checks cashed.

The day after One Eye came, we saw Mr. Kelvin again. He drove up in the jeep and for a while he didn't get out but just sat in it, looking at the house and the barn. I was proud of us and what we had done, but after some time of sitting, Mama sent Jane to ask if he was all right. He looked out at her and said, "It must be the heat—riding up here in all this heat." Then he smiled at her and got out of the jeep and came in, and we gave him a drink of lemonade, making the point that if we were up to all our authenticity on the SCELP, there wouldn't be either the lemons or the ice for that "traditional old-time drink." Mr. Kelvin seemed glad about that. He smiled at us and then relaxed.

"It's what the visitors will need to deal with, to grow with and understand—natural light and darkness and natural work. These things, philosophy, pace, these things are more important than ice and machines and electricity. When—as I came up here and looked out over the hills, I began to imagine—well, never mind, but there's blessing here, recovery, healing, and it makes a man dream . . ."

Daddy said so only I could hear, "Dear God, we've all gone and sold ourselves to a lunatic."

Mama said she thought it was a beautiful sentiment.

Mr. Kelvin walked the place with us, the house and barn and smokehouse and corral and root cellar—not the one under the barn—the one we keep the garden stuff in. At each place we discussed what we could go back to and what we needed to keep, where the old tools would work and where we could at least hide the new ones or use them when the visitors weren't here. Daddy said he would keep the irrigation system and Mama said she'd die with her arms around the washer. Mr. Kelvin said the visitors would do the washing if she had the old boiler the family used to use. Everything was decided and written into a plan Mr. Kelvin made. It covered using the old water pump and when and where we would use our faucets and how we would heat water on the woodstove and all the details of our new authenticity. I thought Mama would cry two or three times. She only sighed and said, "I remember your Daddy's mama telling me about how they got water inside and how excited the women were. I feel like I'm going back on her memory." I saw Louise's mouth starting to open. Mama and Grandma Fleuri never had gotten along, and Louise was about to remind everyone about it, but I stood on her foot in time and she didn't say anything.

So we kept on around to the barn and corral, and then as he was leaving Mr. Kelvin said, "This will work out well—you'll see. Wait until the visitors come. They'll show you how fortunate you are, what a special place this is. A man comes up here and is transported to the past, to a time of simplicity—it expands the mind and rests the soul." We stared at him. He went on. "As I came up this time I looked out over the land and I saw— I imagined I saw the wonderful old-time long-horned cattle of the West, those wonderful herds of the past whose . . ."

We all stopped breathing, and when Mr. Kelvin was finished at last Robert Luther said, "Where did you see these cattle?"

Mr. Kelvin got shy. "Well," he said, "I couldn't really have seen them, could I, but on the road up there's a place where you turn a little and there's a break in the trees, and I thought—I seemed to see them there up on the hill across the gully. I was past the place in a second and I saw them out of the corner of my eye, or thought— dreamed—I saw them. That's not the point, really. The point is that you have here the essence of those days, the very pictures that are made in the mind here, recall those hardy people and stock who were the giants of this land."

Robert Luther smiled and excused himself. We all wished Mr. Kelvin would go right then. One Eye must have left the first gate open when he left and the long-horns must have moved down and through and gone into the gully near the road and then up the hill. Luckily they didn't stop Mr. Kelvin's car on the road. It would not have been so poetic then. They're mean and more than half wild. Everybody got restless and waited for Mr. Kelvin to say his good-byes and leave. I made up an excuse and slipped away to saddle up and go help Robert Luther round them up. Daddy must have stood there with his feet smoking in his shoes. None of us got home until well after dark.

So there we were, niopeers—Louise says that's pi-oneers in the funny kind of pig-Latin she uses—people who go where everybody's already been. "Tell Mama it's all been done before," I said.

Louise said, "Mama never heated her dishwater on

49

a woodstove or had to argue with anyone as to whether the bathtub stayed or went."

"The bathtub does stay!" Mama shouted, "and the hot water for it, and these girls' and my woman's monthly supplies, and that is final!" She was so upset she included Louise and Jane in that, though Jane was probably six years from her period. Niopeers. You should see the papers we had to fill out.

6

One Eye

It's a goddamn crime what people'll do for money—
I'd been takin' Fleuri for so many years, seemed like mine
to do, though he wasn't never no more than pin money
to me, and here come this government bozo working the
biggest scam there is and gotten hold of *my* sucker! It's
enough to weaken a man's hold. Fleuris was always farm-
ers, which in my books says losers. Even when you're
in one of them agribusinesses, you're walkin' in cow shit
and horse shit all day. I don't know how he's hung on
this long. My pa used to sell his pa stuff. Back then I
thought my pa was a fool, that when *I* got to tradin' we'd
throw the land open, grow hemp and poppies, run stuff
that'd pay. They always made a good sippin' whiskey,
the Fleuris did. When my pa died, I went to Fleuri and
tried to get him to increase that output and never mind
the damn cattle or the damn hay, or even the deer he
brought down out of season. He had the grain and the
wood—I was into dreamin' big in them days and here

the damn loser kept saying he wanted to be a rancher who made a little popscull on the side, not a moonshiner who kept stock. Amazin', the pictures people have of themselves. We could have had a four-state operation moonshinin', but a loser don't change. It all come to nothin'.

Over the years I seen big opportunities open up in places where the things come up too quick for big organizations to get to. I always figured a few of those'd be what I wanted—a few big, quick killin's and I'd be made. Now I'm standin' at the edge of the biggest one I ever had and here my supplier goes all strange on me.

Because they found all the stills at the state prison, the ones the prisoners had. I was supplyin' two of the county jails with shine, most of it Fleuri's. One day I'm walkin' Sixteenth and Larimer. I seen Limpin' Charlie, and he tells me he just got out and that the fuzz found their still and broke it up and found the route the stuff took—found how the ingredients got there—and broke *that* up. So now two thousand thirsty cons got nothin' but what the three bribable guards will let in. It's the goddamn chance of a lifetime. I had some stuff in the truck. Coke. I give him a line and jump in the truck and head out for the hills. My hands was shakin' when I started it up, and drivin' I started to laugh; opportunity is knockin', but it's so shaky with the D.T.'s it can't hit my door. Never mind, I hear it anyway. I'm thinkin' hard, countin' things up. Some of it is hard to live with.

1. Harlan Jenks, who makes good booze, is a boozer himself and lately his product ain't been dependable. There's been dirt in it, and stuff on the bottom.

2. The Catlins. They skipped to escape a warrant.

3. Malloy, the printer, never made more than ten gallons at a run. It's good—there just ain't enough of it. Everybody's gone to dope and stopped makin' booze at

52

all. In six months or so, the cons' own still will be back in operation. The opportunity is now, in and out quick.

I was thinkin' all about this when I turned off to Bascom and started up Fleuri's damn axle-buster of a mountain. It was gonna take some kind of story, too. Fleuri wouldn't want to put himself out for no cons. I had somethin' worked out by the time I got up there.

Fleuri and Kate was in the corral with a horse and four of his rangy cows. I walked up careful; we started jokin' and talkin' and then I got ready to lay my story on him. For some reason, the girls and Robert Luther was in odd-lookin' costumes and that put me off. It's hard to talk to people in costumes. I looked at Akin and seen his clothes were more than just old. His pants had a buttoned fly. I started to laugh and he said all it did was to make you plan ahead a little more. I just stood there and at first I thought they was kiddin', but I seen they really taken all their old junk from the back of the barn, the binders and cutters and a sledge, and they was actually gettin' 'em ready to use. They wasn't kiddin' at all. They started to talk about this government scheme they was on, about bein' back in the 1880s and havin' people visit 'em to live the life that was goin' on back then. They proved it was true, all of it. I had to sit down and think about what all this was gonna mean to me.

How was Fleuri gonna keep his shebang work from visitors, government people, wanderin' inspectors, and who-shot-John any time of day? I never paid no taxes—state or federal—but I got angry thinkin' that program would end up keepin' me from *my* popscull and *my* business. It's enough to turn a man against the government. Eighteen eighty. I couldn't believe it. Now, when I needed the poor hayseed to produce for two thousand thirsty cons . . .

Later Fleuri admitted they weren't actually payin'

him, not money in his hand. He'd need extra cash somewhere. That knowledge said *shebang.*

So, we talked about it. He said the visitors wouldn't
be there all the time. Whenever they weren't there, he
and Robert Luther could concentrate on the shebang
and that would guarantee us our forty gallons a run—
the same two runs a year.

So it was time to pull out my story. "See, this vets'
group is my old battalion, and they started havin' reun-
ions—you know how it is, a bunch of guys sittin' around
and talkin' about the old days in Korea. I guess I bragged.
I told 'em I knew where they could get the best sippin'
whiskey made. I even give 'em some samples I didn't
sell. They took up on it right away and they want it—
both battalions I used to belong to, for drinkin' after our
weekly meetin's." I went on like that. I told Fleuri we'd
need more—double what he was producin' now and for
at least six or seven months, until I could find some other
sources and ease up on him.

I told him I'd up his price per gallon. I argued that
now it was summer he might get in an extra run before
the big work of the ranch had to be done. I knew the
cash was temptin'. . . . He said he didn't know how busy
they'd be now they were havin' to do so much without
usin' any modern equipment. I guess I lost my temper.
I said some things and stomped off, but business is business. I come back a week later and told 'em my Korean
vet story again. Just when we all could have been rich!
Just when things could have been bigger than they were
in 1972 when I was runnin' marijuana and hash to the
junior college. What was the matter with these people?
I knew I had to go slow now I had blown up at Fleuri
in front of his kids.

Every time I seen 'em they had gone back more. The
clothes and the farm equipment, piece by piece; the sunbonnets and straw hats, the long skirts and the aprons,

horse harnesses and spring wagons. I seen 'em changin' week by week as I come to help take the grain up to the ferment vats and check out the product. There was something takin' about them, even Mary Beth, that blimp, looked better wearin' long clothes in them soft colors—flowin'. The girls was lettin' their hair grow long, and though they tied it up for work, I knew it could be brushed out long and straight to shine down their shoulders. The woman I had downtown started to look kinda hard-boned to what Croom's women were.

But they was wastin' time that should have been spent out at the shebang, runnin' product. I seen that government man now and then and once I met him on the road and had to back down half a damn mile before I found a pull-off so he could pass. When I come up and he was there, we talked around him in a kind of code. Ugly comes in handy for my kind of work. The man was too scared to look at me and too polite to ask about me, which was how I have always gotten by with cops, social workers, wardens, screws, and parole officers. I kept tellin' Fleuri, "For the first time, we got customers eager and waitin'—rooms full of 'em!" I never told him all them rooms had bars down one side.

I admit this. What I done come back on me. Maybe fifteen years ago I got scared Fleuri was gonna ask for more money, so I dreamed up eight, ten other makers, and I would let him know how good *they* was doin' and how happy *they* was with "standard price." Now, Robert Luther says, "You'll have to get your other producers to gear up." I put a hurt look on and turned my good eye away and said, "Young Robert Luther, suppose you let your daddy do the talkin'." It had worked before, but since this SCELP thing and all of them at one fever pitch over it, Akin seemed to have give over something to Robert Luther. Now he said, "Let's keep things like they been. We've been puttin' up the same two runs a year since I can remember," but I did get 'em to promise an extra run. It wasn't enough—not near enough—and with all the times I been comin' up this damn mountain, my truck was startin' to shake apart . . .

For a while I thought there might be a way I could ruin the SCELP thing for the Fleuris; then I could have 'em do the job them and their stupid ranch was meant to do. I thought of callin' in their names to SCELP for bootleggin' whiskey and sellin' illegal deer, but none of it could be done without blowin' my own cover. I thought someone could plant drugs in Miss Kate's locker at school. Even these rubes know what cocaine is. I give that one a lot of thought. Certain guys owe me favors, and it'd be fun to get Miss Pretty Pants up to her nose in front of her town friends. Maybe Robert Luther might end up with heroin in his truck. I seen that wouldn't work—I need 'em to work the shebang, not to be in jail. Akin. *Sleepin'*. Who drops down like a sack of grain in the middle of a sentence? I always figured he was havin' some kind of a still fit—I seen regular fits—this was just a still one, except at the end his eyes pop open and like nothin' happened he gets up and goes back to work or tellin' the story. How could I fix that to work with the SCELP people? They'd have to see one, but I don't know when they come or when the fits do.

In the meantime, I give what I had to Randy Madison and Peachy—forty gallons of moonshine, which they will cut again, probably, and resell very well at the prison. I spent the whole week touring like the Greyhound bus company to get more. Everybody wants to drink it; no one wants to make it.

Three weeks later I was back up Fleuri's awful road. Someone had been by and put up crushed stone in the worst places, but the truck still bucked and pitched. I didn't care. I had to try one more time to talk Fleuri out of this government business or into more runs.

When I come up over the rise of the land, suddenly, I seen what the government man must have seen in his mind—him and Fleuri, too. It looked like a damn Christmas card. They had put the porch back and gotten rid of the lean it had. They had painted the house and the porch and put back the little roof ding-ey that I had forgotten had been there long ago and they had made the old-fashioned eave stops that had been there. It was beautiful, kind of—like a picture. The barn, too, was painted nice and reshingled. It didn't look hip-shot no more—I guess it was all braced and I saw right off that it was *that* barn and *that* house and not the people at all that had taken the government man.

I started in my story again. "These vets get together and they're all wounded and they want to sit around and talk about them times they went through and then they want to set up some authentic American sippin's—none of that bottled, pasteurized, sterilized stuff—American stuff like they fought and bled for." I done everything but break out with "The Star-Spangled Banner." When I got through, all they could promise me was somethin' in October, and a delivery in between visitors. "I can't run any more than my setup will do," Akin kept sayin'.

"What if I help you get more setup, something more modern? Sort of SCELP in reverse?"

Akin was shakin' his head. "It still takes the time it takes."

So here I am, waitin' on 'em to screw up on this government joke, which they will; and here I am, waitin' on that ranch to go down the tubes, which it will; and here I am, talkin' sense to a bunch of nitwits in costumes; and here I am, stuck, stopped, waitin' for somethin' I can use to ruin 'em, and a jail full of thirsty cons waitin' on *me*. Why does everything open up and then shut on my neck when I go to walk through? Why does it all spring holes for me?

7

Mary Beth

It's six P.M. in the evenin'. The cocktails has all been given out, but the dancin' don't start till nine. It's summer and still light. I guess it's always summer at my parties. Later, when it gets dark, there'll be Japanese lanterns, but now there's a yellow haze on everything. The ladies are in long summer gowns and they seem to float around on the lawns. Underneath big trees some of them are sittin' and talkin' and laughin'. They are all famous and they all know each other because famous people read the papers, too. There is music—happy-sad music, and champagne and little delicate food—stuff you hear about and never eat, like caviar and truffles. These is world-famous people like is on our wall. In my parties I always have people who do wonderful things all the time and who are at my mansion restin' from their greatness. "Kate," I say from the kitchen, "I'm gonna send limousines after the party and not let these folks drive themselves home." I think that's a real nice end to a party, don't you?

I was born here, raised here, married in the church in Bascom, and I'll probably die in this place. It sounds sad, but I like Bascom, or used to, and I love my family and Croom Mountain.

I guess I was a big disappointment to Ma and Pa. Big is right. I'm heavy, always was, and not very smart or pretty or anything a girl is supposed to be. Even hair. A fat girl can get by if she got good hair, but mine is mud-brown and frizzy and kind of thin. There was five of us: Cassie had a nice smile; Frances's teeth were lovely; Bud was a stocky boy. He went into the military. Selena was petite and quick in her movements, and then me, comin' last. It seemed like all the gifts, the riches, had been give out before I got there and nothing was left and Ma and Pa just said, well, that's that.

But it come to me one day that all the while I wasn't *bein'* beautiful, I was seein' beautiful things all around me. That made me happy all through a whole life of bein' plain. I could hear any kind of story and exactly imagine the people it was happening to. I went all through school makin' all that history and geography and English into stories, until the teachers was wore out with me.

Akin Fleuri was the only person I ever met who didn't laugh at me outright. That's a big part of the reason I married him. I guess people laughed at him for doing it, but they laughed at him anyway because of his sleepin' habit that most people—even his folks—thought of as a kind of disgrace. Akin's a good man, fits or no fits, and we got used to being what we are. Akin's daddy left us the ranch because he said we weren't neither of us fit for no better.

What happened then was a kind of a miracle. Akin and me had one, two, three, four kids, all beautiful, quick, smart, and handy. If a scientist was to look down at our genetics, Akin's and mine, he would scratch his head for two hours and go away and tear up his books. Watchin' 'em grow, I couldn't hardly believe my eyes: day by day, year by year, Robert Luther and then Kate, Louise, and then Jane, come on without any help from us, like the ideas and grace was inside them all along. Where did they get the account they drew on? Sure, I talked to 'em and read and we had TV then and radio, but it wasn't like smartness *goin' in*, it was like smartness *comin' out*, and I'd watch and rub my eyes and listen again and wonder how their handsomeness and beauty come when it wasn't nothin' on either side of our families but fits and starts back to God knows when.

When Robert Luther was nine years old, he come to me and says, "You know, Mama, Daddy sleeps regular; his sleeps come seven hours apart and they last just fifteen minutes, and then the seven hours begins again and that's why they seem to come all different times. But they're regular as any clock." Well, I timed it and it was true, and then Robert Luther said, "Because we can predict Daddy's sleep . . ." and he used that word, *predict*. Nine years old, and me that had grown up with Akin never noticin', or his family neither. It was only then I knew that Akin must have sensed the sleeps was steady, regular someway, in a rhythm that let him protect himself.

It was Robert Luther who changed the direction of the old irrigation system and who found ways to have more efficiency around the place. At first Akin wouldn't listen—Robert Luther being only a boy then—but smart idea after smart idea and Akin had to follow Robert Luther's advice. Once in town I heard Mr. Carmer say, when he thought I was gone, "How could such a brainless twit have such smart kids?" and that like to made me die of pride.

Kate is smart, and her smartness has to do with people. Town kids never laugh at her like they done at me.

60

They like her. Everyone in town does, too, even the new, richer people in Crestmore and Meadow View, even though *we* don't fit in in Bascom. It's a miracle to me.

Louise is smartest in school things. She keeps a diary and writes down all her impressions. She wrote the school play last year. It was about the discovery of fire.

Jane is only six but she's like a fairy-child—she glows. She's darker than the others were at her age; her eyes are dark and they shine when she's happy 'til your heart wants to break with it.

And all this to me—to us: the dull, fat girl and the sleeping boy that even in their growin' years when everyone seems dream-lit, never shone.

I remember us back in our high school days. I tell the girls a lot of things, but not this—it hurts too much. Years ago, the first years of high school, I liked to be in town. There was ranch kids in Bascom then, kids like we was, who knew about calf weaning and rounding up and gelding and branding. We would go to town, shoppin', and meet them there and stop and talk for a minute and have things to say without feeling silly. When Akin and I got married, our friends was interested because we was almost the first. We was proud. I showed off my gold band a little—you know, like kids'll do.

But after high school, one by one the ranch kids and the town kids left, and some even died. There was auto accidents and huntin' accidents; people got married and moved away. Some went to college and never really come back, and I had a feelin' of bein' left behind like a piece of paper or a rag the wind caught on a bush—stuck here.

None of the girls or Robert Luther has ever laughed at me for visitin' all those stately homes, but I know deep down that if I really lived in one of 'em, the neighbors would laugh at me a sight more than people do here. It's why I don't move away to any foreign place like Paris,

France, or London, England, for any more than a quick visit. It's because I know that if I went to any of them places, I would seem real simple to them people and they would laugh and it would kind of reflect bad on America—you know—people would think all of us was as dumb as I am.

With all we had to do, the month of August was lost in work. The men cut hay and tried to use the old machines for part of it to see how they worked, and the learnin' took time and was a awful trial to Akin. Robert Luther worked so hard I could see him almost ready to fall asleep in his food at night. The girls and I was busy enough, but Kate, who was a good hand, worked the stock and spent time at the shebang, which I do not approve. Girls and women should not be involved in product. It was my daddy's rule. I think it's unfeminine for girls, anyway. Kate says I'm old-fashioned in that, but old-fashioned is just what we need to be, ain't it? It's a new word now, and I learned it from Mr. Kelvin. *Authentic.* I said to Kate, "I'm authenic, is what."

Every now and then Mr. Kelvin come, seein' us and okayin' things as we got ready for our visitors, gettin' more and more authentic. Once he come when I was pluckin' a turkey—we thought we'd raise a few of 'em along with our chickens. I was workin' hard, buried up to my neck in wet feathers that was stickin' to me and in my hair and up my nose and half the bird still to do, and he nods and smiles and then he says, "I see you are still in that red dress . . ."

"Easier with the bird," I say, "throw 'er in the wash and all the sweat and feathers is a memory. Polyester."

"Fails on the authenticity, though."

"No one's here yet . . ."

"Yes, but you need to get used to wearing the work clothes to do the work." So the polyester has to go.

Mr. Kelvin said the idea of our parlor wall was authentic, but not the wall itself. He put in for old-timey papers that he said we could cover with a special spray to make 'em last. New technology, he said, but one that didn't show. I know we'll miss our wall friends, the runners and the President and them two doctors, Masters and Johnson, who the paper says are at the "cutting edge of research in a field much spoken of but rarely studied." I like them because they look like good, stern old-time grandparents, only wearin' hospital coats instead of regular clothes. We put the names under all of them for the kids to learn.

Kate had a dream two nights before the orientation people come. I know because it was a nightmare and it woke us up when she screamed out loud. We got her back to sleep, but the next day she told me it was about her bein' in the parlor and there not bein' a door in it. We'd papered over the door somehow. The President and Alvin Ailey, Dr. Masters, and Dr. Johnson was angry about her havin' left their century. It's just Kate bein' nervous about the orientation people. I'm nervous, too. I'm afraid that some mess of mine might keep all of us from bein' on the SCELP. The orientation people was coming to show us how to have visitors and fill out all their papers and everything. They was goin' to stay a week, and Mr. Kelvin said they was only there to help us and that we shouldn't be nervous, but I was still pretty scared and I wanted everything to be nice. On Wednesday, we went to shop in Bascom. It gave me a last chance to wear my bright clothes and be not authentic.

Town. Years ago Akin and I got so we went to Bascom, did our shopping, and come back quick as we could. As soon as I got to realize that folks was laughin' at us, our looks and our ways, I stopped feelin' good about goin'.

Bascom has changed a lot, all the suburban develop-
ments and their people. Kate and the kids may like town
but I hardly know anybody there anymore; there is only
a few older people I see, the others like us who stayed
on after good sense told 'em their times was over. Down
in Bascom it always come to me about my hair being
wrong and my clothes and my size, my walk, my shoes,
my education, my job, our car, and our lives.

Akin leaves the kids off to go to friends' houses. Their
friends take turns runnin' 'em back home. Then he drives
me to the shopping mall to grocery shop while he goes
to the lumberyard or the hardware store or the auto parts.
This time we had a lot of last things we wanted to get
before the orientation people come and did their report
on us. I got some notions, buttons and things at the
drugstore, and went into the supermarket, determined,
like I always am, not to take too long. I had a list and a
bunch of coupons and was tryin' to be efficient. But the
labels got me. The labels always do.

I love the labels on the sanitary-napkin boxes and
the cat-food boxes and especially the herb-tea boxes at
the end of aisle 8. I love the dreams they show. The
sanitary-napkin-box girl is runnin' along the seashore
kickin' up spray. She's beautiful and her hair trails out
behind her. I love that picture because it doesn't show
too much, but you know how she feels, runnin' along
that way on a good day in a beautiful place. I always stop
at that box and look at that girl runnin'. The cat-food
boxes show the cutest cats you can imagine, but the tea
is where I have to stop and stand. Starry nights on Arab
towers, secret, mossy places where trails go away among
the trees, apple branches in blossom—it's all so pretty
it's hard to tear yourself away, hard to imagine how
anybody could have imagined them, palaces and castles
and all. I swear every week I won't stop but I always do,
and Akin gets angry because sometimes he has to come

and get me, standin' there in the gardens of the palace or in the starflower grove waitin' for—

"Why, hello, Mrs. Fleuri . . ." And I could have cried. I was caught there, starin' at the tea, and with my list not half done, lookin' like a nitwit. Who was it? I turned around. It was Mrs. Francis, the secretary at the elementary school. I noticed she must have been on her way to the checkout because her cart was full. I said, "Hello." To my surprise, she didn't walk past. Instead she said, "Well, how are *you*?" I said, "Fine." I couldn't figure it out. Of course she knew the kids but she never done any more than nod to me when I come to school or saw her in town. She said, "Isn't it exciting what's happened? Everyone is so interested!" I wondered what she was talkin' about, what I had missed. Everything looked the same. It's hard to stand and wait to hear the news everyone else is in on. "I know you're proud for the kids," she said, "but you're probably worried about all the attention they'll get, especially when school starts again in the fall. I can tell you those kids of yours won't be changed a bit by any of it."

I heard the word *kids*, my kids, and I guess I stopped hearin' at all. Mrs. Francis went on talkin'—I seen her lips move but I was just in a panic for a minute. I said, "Kids—what about the kids?" and I made myself listen until I heard her say, "Why, the program you're all on. One of the children—Jane, I think—mentioned it to my Serena and I guess Serena told her friends. I saw Kate last week and got the story from her. I think it's wonderful, your family and the ranch being selected that way."

I said, "Oh—" and didn't know what else to say. She went on about how good it was, and about the kind of people who would come, scientists and writers and celebrities and that. I wanted to tell her we hadn't had anyone yet and the first ones who was coming was only going to be orientation people, but I thought if I did that, it would make Jane and Kate out to be liars. Mrs. Francis said, "Who are you getting next?" I was relieved to be able to say, "People are coming tomorrow—I don't know their names yet."

She came close and whispered, "Who is it? Can you tell me?" and I was about to say somethin' and then I remembered that Mr. Kelvin told us that we were not supposed to tell who it was and I said, "We have to keep confidential, but maybe later when the program gets more under way, the kids can have their regular hayride with some of the visitors."

She said, "Well, yes," and was looking into my basket to see what I was getting and I said, "I guess i have to go now." I was turning away when another woman whose face I knew but whose name I didn't passed by and said, "Hello, Mary Beth, how are you today?" and I smiled at her.

It took me a hour and a half to get out of the store. Mrs. Bodine stopped me, and the Kennedys, talkin' about the program, askin' about what we was doin' and was we goin' to have a cattle drive in town like they used to do a hundred years ago. Mrs. Race said hello. People who had always give me the go-by even though our kids have gone to school together—there they were now remindin' me of it and sayin' "How's Kate?" "How's Robert Luther?"

Before I could think a minute, there I was tellin' people about the 1880s, about how cookin' on a wood-stove was so hot on summer noons you couldn't hardly stand it, about how the toaster on the stand had to be watched like a hawk or you'd have charcoal in an eye-blink. They listened and I opened up like I haven't since I was in high school and me and Akin was goin' together. They'd say "Really . . ." and "I never thought about that." I told 'em about how fireplace ash was gettin' to be more

66

of a need than the fire that made it—for makin' lye and for sanitation in the privy. "Making your own lye?" Mrs. Bodine said.

By that time there was a little crowd around me and their carts was pulled in like cows at the water ring, kind of bumpin' easy side to side, companionable.

"Lord, yes—Robert Luther has had to make a percolator box or box with fine screen on the bottom so the rain water can run down through the ash and then rerun, and that's settled out and there's your lye-water."

Then Mrs. Francis said, "I bet you're proud of being part of that—it's so interesting . . ."

I told 'em all about the sausage makers we cleaned up and the churns we steam-cleaned and the presses and hand-cranked this and that. I told 'em what was in my mind. I didn't say what was on my heart, that spirits of Akin's grandma and hers before her was wringin' their hands that I remember all knobbed and scarred, hissin' "fool of this world" in my ears for all the way they'd come and that I was betrayin' them somehow and betrayin' Kate and Louise and Jane. I didn't say a word of that.

I realized in the middle that Akin was sure to be waitin' in the truck, seething mad. I was wonderin', too, all the time I answered questions about the SCELP and said hello to people, why he hadn't come lookin' for me with blood in his eye. I was a celebrity all of a sudden, and celebrities have to move real slow. I kept expectin' him to roar in any minute and find me roundin' the aisle between tuna fish and cake flour, his hat stuffed down on his head, ready to say "What's kept you, woman," but he didn't come and I was enjoyin', really enjoyin', bein' such a celebrity. Mrs. Bodine and Mrs. Francis drifted away and I walked on but I still got stopped by four or five people to say hello and answer questions and, "Yes, Thursday is my regular day, but I'm here today because people are comin' tomorrow."

The kids had been braggin' maybe, but shouldn't town be like this—friendly and curious in a nice way? I thought after all these years it didn't matter to me if people greeted me or not, but all of a sudden I felt younger, lighter, talking to them, answering questions about the SCELP. I was surprised that so many people had heard of it. Some of them even known about programs in other states, and that for some of the real popular ones you could only go by lottery. They said the American Indian ones were like that. I felt cheerful, not tired at all when I left the store and I walked out to the parking lot and tried to pick out our truck down the row. It wasn't there. For a while I stood and stared for it, gettin' scared that somethin' had happened to Akin, but then I saw it turnin' into the shopping center and comin' toward me. I waved, but Akin didn't see me. It was too far to call. I saw him pull into a slot and turn the motor off. Then he got out and I started walkin' toward him with my shopping cart. He saw me then, but instead of stoppin', he kept on walkin'. He was different. He didn't look like the same man. I realized that it was the way he was walkin', his head up, his arms—they was—I remembered twenty years ago, that habit of his, a kind of swing, a little extra swing he had to his arms and a little rock to his step. He was doin' that now, that little swing. He seen me comin' and stopped to watch me. I could see in his face that I had changed, too, that my head was up and that I wasn't standin' behind my cart huddlin' sort of, the way I guess I do in town. I smiled at him. I never smile at him in town, across a distance like that. Both of us was actin' real funny and what was even funnier was that we could still surprise each other after all these years. When I come up to him, he says, "Mary Beth, you're an idiot."

I said, "Yes, I know."

"This town's OK is twenty years too late."

"I'll take it anytime."

"Why don't it make you tearin' mad? Where's your dignity?"

"But they're like kids—you can't get mad at kids for what they done yesterday. You have to live every day new with a kid."

"How do you mean they're like kids?"

"Because they don't even see they been doin' something they shouldn't."

"How do you know?"

"If they did see, they'd be ashamed and they're not."

"So you just take it."

"Akin, bein' happy has always beat bein' sad."

"Herman Jaspers kept me talkin' down at the hardware. The Kelley kid. Sam Bodine. *Sam Bodine*, mind you, who offered me a dollar an acre for the Croom five years ago, to put up a dog cemetery or some damn thing. Now he says bein' SCELP is like bein' a National Park, and the land values'll rise all over the area because of it. Thanks to us. Said we should have cards printed. I said somethin' should be printed on his hind end."

"But it made you happy, didn't it? I can see it in your face right now."

"It makes me mad."

I didn't tell him the other thing I knew, that it's better to be mad than sad and better to be mad than scared and draggy the way we both been in town all these years.

That evening when we got home I told Kate about it—not the way we felt, but about how people had greeted us, all the people in the grocery store, people who never had before, because of the SCELP, and she said, "You deserve that, Mama, you always did." That night when I went outside to put the stove ash in the lye box, I didn't hear my grandma's ghost hissin' the waste of all her years on the little night breeze or Akin sayin' "You're an idiot" beside me.

So we got ready for visitors and we was nervous and excited like before the school play, and the ranch looked like 1880, and so did we in our new old-timey clothes, and our new long hair, and when a plane flew over us next morning early, Jane yelled up at it, "You can't fly over here—this is an old-timey place!" and we all laughed.

8

Orientation Report

NAME OF PLACEMENT:
Croom Ranch, "The Croom."
Year: 1880–1887

NAMES OF ENABLING PARTIES:
Fleuri, Akin, 40;
Fleuri, Mary Beth, 40;
Fleuri, Robert Luther, 18;
Fleuri, Kate, 15;
Fleuri, Louise, 12;
Fleuri, Jane, 6.

NAME OF FIELD COUNSELOR:
J. M. Kelvin

DATE OF ORIENTATION PLACEMENT:
September 1–7

INVENTORY SHEETS 1–7 ARE APPENDED.

PERSONAL COMMENTS:

Because of the season (see above), most of the work was farm rather than ranch work. The cattle were pasturing on the highest hills, their calves, born earlier in the spring, with them. Hay was cut, grain was cut and bagged, corn was harvested, and some of it was sprouted as was the wheat to be malted for extra nutrition. The cutting was done with a horse-drawn combine that the three of us managed, although there were quite a few breakdowns. Requisitions for machining the necessary spare parts are appended. An electric-powered pump is supplying irrigation water, which the enabling parties refuse to relinquish. Perhaps next year we can get them to go back to a wind-powered pump. Aside from this small concession to the twentieth century, the authenticity is high. There are horses to be harnessed and cared for, fed and watered, farm work of all kinds, and later in the year, the slaughtering of the cattle with extant implements and the canning and processing of meat, soap making, et cetera.

Akin Fleuri: Mr. Fleuri is a rather gruff individual, but this fits well with the patriarchal mode of the time. I wish we could get him to give up some of the personal idiosyncrasies he demands be saved—two-track shaver, et cetera. He also curses a good deal, and because Croom is a family placement, care will have to be taken in this regard. He is of a somewhat secretive manner, but we have been unable to learn what he was hiding, in effect, to "get anything on him." He has on occasion expressed wonder and not a little scorn at our acceptance of our part of the work load. However, scornful as he was, he asked our male worker to sign on as a hired hand at the rate of five dollars a day for the season. The worker asked him if those were 1880 wages, and he voiced a common expletive.

Mary Beth Fleuri: Mrs. Fleuri is still quite confused about the program. We almost had to pull her light, inauthentic plastic wash pails and dishpans from her hands, and she was on the point of tears when we replaced them with the heavier wood-and-metal things from the cooperage. Periodically, she is still requesting awnings and Japanese lanterns, although we have told her we are completely unable to authenticate the presence of these things on any of the foothill or plains ranches of the 1880s. Mrs. Fleuri has made a very great effort to cook authentically on the stoves provided, using authentic utensils and following the regional Victorian menu and methods of food preparation. She is, however, a terrible cook, unless, of course, it's authentically terrible. Please call a conference of food experts on this matter. We tried to find out if she was a terrible cook before SCELP. She is very friendly, though, and does not resent efforts to help. We discussed the possibility that some of the pioneer women of the day might not have been completely stalwart and dependable. Could an intellectually deprived person have survived in pioneer days? Please advise.

Robert Luther is the strongest and most willing member of the group. He is a hard worker, an excellent teacher, and is both patient and encouraging. He has, however, spent a good deal of his personal requisition money on a bewildering variety of hats and headgear and on what might be called costume accessories, gaiters, spats, chaps, et cetera. This, before the program has even begun.

Kate Fleuri is a very strong asset to the group. While somewhat less patient than Robert Luther, she is sure to be a good role model for young people who come on the program. She is punctilious about authenticity and has great powers of charm and personal attractiveness.

Louise and *Jane* are children but seemed helpful and pleasant. They work positively and are interested in the success of the SCELP program.

The female worker found the Fleuris self-conscious, which she assumes will ease with time. The children seem nervous for both the father and mother, the parents for the children. One wonders if this, too, was authentic for 1880, when isolation forged stronger family ties in a dangerous environment. Perhaps we should worry more about the effect of outsiders on this family than vice versa.

Problems with capital formation, insurance, and isolation late in season are covered in appended sections of this report.

9

Louise

I have always had two lives; one inside and one outside. My problem has always been to get more of the inside one. When I learned to read I saw that books were stronger for me and had more colors than the world and that the pictures in my mind were more interesting to examine and try to put words to. Now that we are on SCELP there are four worlds, not two. The third world is the world of 1880. The fourth world is one I know better than the rest of my family. It has to do with holding out.

In clothing: shoes. The long dresses are soft and layered with petticoats, and they are easy on our bodies. Even with the wide skirts you can climb a tree or a ladder or ride a horse, but shoes do not forgive. Mama goes barefoot in the house while it's still summer, but when the cold comes she'll have to get some kind of slippers because she says the six-button shoe is the torturer's treat. Jane keeps her tennies until thirty seconds before the visitors come and then she wears moccasins from the Pay-Less, because the Indians invented the moccasin. Kate and Robert Luther tried the catalogues and ended up with a kind of boot, a work boot. We all greet the visitors in those damn button things, and then we go back, holding out. I go barefoot, get stone bruises, and end up with what the catalogue calls pattens. That and three pairs of socks will be my winter. Mama holds out for brassieres and no corset. "Let 'em come and take this bra off my dead body! Let the FBI!" But she has to wash it secretly and hang it in the attic to dry. The wash line has to be authentic. Everyone holds out for toilet paper instead of corncobs or straw, and Mama and Kate use Kotex instead of rags you wash and use over again. Mama is currently in mourning for her detergent. She has to use bar soap for the dishes and the stuff leaves a whitish grease-sweat on everything, and you have to use a vinegar rinse to get it off.

When will I get time to read at all? It takes all day for me and the visiting kids to go out with wood wagons and get the fallen branches and cut them to size to heat our water and cook our food. The wash-boilers eat wood like locomotives. The water has to be heated and carried up to the bathtubs and the old water carried out, and we use each other's bath water. So we shower, which is NA (not authentic).

People never use most of the words there are for them, words like *egregious*, *deracinated*, *cancrazantic*. Those words are like the herbs and spices they sell in the fancy stores in town—shelves of them that change the flavor of food a dozen ways. When will I have time to learn those words, to taste them, now that I am carrying water here and there? Wood in and ashes out, water in and water out.

I suppose I am learning other things. Kate told the orientation people that the sprouted malted grain was for calves' nutrition. They believed her. It was a fabrication. The malted grain was for product. One Eye (egregious) made Daddy promise, I think, to do another run of product. Suddenly we seem to need a lot more money than we did. This had to do with possibilities. I am on the edge of learning something very important about hope— the bad side of it—but I don't have the words for it yet. When will I get the chance to think about these things?

Mr. Kelvin comes up on surprise visits, sometimes. Last time he caught me reading *Island of the Blue Dolphins*, a *beautiful* book. I get my books ten at a time from the library in Bascom. The book is NA. So are Chekhov's short stories, *Old Yeller, David Copperfield, Jane Eyre*, and nine-tenths of everything I read or want to read. When we go to shop in Bascom I spend my time in the library, making my selections. Last time I took my problem to Mrs. Patterson and Mrs. Boyd at the library. We got ten titles that were authentic for young girls to read out here in 1880 and I made oilcloth covers with the titles on them and put them on my ten-a-week books, which are now down to three or four. *This* is called verisimilitude. Punctilious verisimilitude.

Once or twice when Mr. Kelvin was up, One Eye would be here, too. Daddy and One Eye had to begin a code around the visitors and the SCELP people.

DADDY: "That cow drench you sold us was bad."

ONE EYE: "What was the matter with it?"

DADDY: "Smell is off. I won't use it on my stock. You'll have to take back all forty gallons."

ONE EYE: "Where is it? Let me see it."

DADDY: "It ain't here. It's up on the range. It's in the shed up there."

ONE EYE: "When would you be usin' it?"

DADDY: "End of September."

ONE EYE: "Mind if I check it out?"

DADDY: "Suit yourself."

Then One Eye would go up to the shebang and see the run coming, or bring the mason jars and old bottles he had brought for the product Daddy had finished. We had all worked that out. We were proud of solving it. We were proud of being able to keep the popscull a secret. We were proud of being able to keep the longhorns secretly over the hill and, after the near-miss with Mr. Kelvin, hidden away, like the book says, "At the back of the north wind." Daddy's sleeps were the hardest thing to keep from visitors.

People think the sleeps are strange. I grew up with them so they only seem ordinary for Daddy, but after we were accepted on SCELP, Robert Luther called a meeting of the kids and explained to us why it was important to protect Daddy from the visitors.

1. That going over in the middle of a meal, on the way somewhere, even in the middle of a word, made people nervous about Daddy's mind.

2. What Daddy did made people nervous about trusting him with cutters, mowers, and other equipment that was unfamiliar to them anyway.

3. That Daddy didn't like people noticing his sleeps.

4. That Daddy's sleeps were not part of SCELP, but private and not for visitors. They were like Maupassant's short stories, which I had started to read in a cover called *A Young Lady's Guide to Conduct and Deportment*.

We began counting from sleep to sleep and making sure the sleeps were regular. They were. I thought Daddy could look out for himself, but Kate and Robert Luther explained to me how funny that would seem: "There they'd be in the middle of doing something—harnessing horses or watering stock—and Daddy would have to say,

'Excuse me, I've got to go right away.' It would seem odd. No one stops regular work ordinarily to do something else unless he has forgotten to do it before. How often should that happen? But if *we* called him, it would be more natural and easy to explain. People often call you from other things."

"Daddy doesn't like to think about his sleeps, does he?"

Robert Luther shook his head. "No, he didn't even show much interest when I told him they were regular, almost by the clock. Too many whippings when he was a kid, I think."

"Too much fuss," Kate said.

"Too much Bascom," I said.

So we agreed, and every day the visitors were there or expected, we would keep track, coming down for breakfast to make a quick plan. "Nine-thirty and quarter-to-four. I'll come out and tell him the binderblades are stuck at nine-fifteen. You go tell him one of the horses looks foundered at three-thirty." It worked pretty well and we were proud because it was a thing we kids were doing on our own. Even Jane was part of it because she might be sent with a message if we were busy. We practiced with her and she acted as proud as a hall monitor in school, standing up, reciting: "Daddy, the pig has gotten stuck in the fence. Robert Luther says to come right away." Sometimes Jane is too cute to live: egregiously cute. Sometimes she really is cute; that time was one of them.

We had several bad moments with all our secrets to protect. One of the longhorns got gored down near the river and Robert Luther had to kill it. He and Daddy cut off its head and skinned it and brought it in, saying it was bred stock and hoping the visitors didn't notice any difference in size. Daddy wasn't happy about teaching us to lie and hide and be clever. I could see how that part bothered him most. Before, I guess he thought all the lies were his alone to tell; now they were family lies. He thought he had protected us better than that. Of course it wasn't so. You don't look at what you don't want to see.

The first actual visitors were a family from New York City. He was a stockbroker, which is *not* someone who deals in cattle, and his wife was a writer's agent, and they had three kids—two girls and a boy. Their name was Lundgren, and both sets of their grandparents had come from farm ranches in Wyoming and Montana. They said they had always been interested in that life. They came with books full of pictures and the family records with stories about the Jespersons and the Lundgrens. They stayed two weeks and worked so hard we were all amazed. They made soap and helped move the stock and cut out the calves for weaning. They flea-treated the chickens and harvested, and the women washed and canned. They were so good, such nice people; Daddy said he wished he could take John Lundgren down the draw and show him the longhorns, the true, old Wyoming stock itself, with none of the brains or meanness or wit of them bred out. They looked so peaceful grazing by the river, but they could turn a sudden field of spears on wolves or coyotes, and they were almost wild for all Daddy's care of them—American, like Mr. Kelvin said all the time, authentic.

Calf weaning is the most nerve-racking time in ranch life. The spring calves are separated from their mothers and brought to the corral and their mothers are taken away upwind of them, out to the farthest field. All day and all night for a week, the calves bawl and cry, and the people on the ranch have no choice but to listen to the sound of them, crying for their mothers. It's hard for anyone to bear, and the Lundgrens had the worst of it, lying in bed at night while crying like all the ghosts that ever were assailed them—assailed and oppressed them on the night wind. They came down in the mornings all sleepless, the first three days of their second week. We could see they were suffering with a kind of pride, all of them, until the hard work of the ranch clubbed them to sleep on the fourth night. They were grateful for all of it; it was pioneer and part of them, they said—heritage.

It was hard to see them leave when their two weeks were over. It came to us as we were sitting around the table the evening they'd gone, that that was what would happen with all the good visitors we had, that SCELP would be more and more authentic in things, but that the feelings—the difficulty of hello and the wrench of good-bye—were a very modern thing, and not "authentic" at all. We were NA in that. The visitors were NA in that, coming and going away, passing by, passing through. It made everyone sad to think about that. Jane cried, but it was probably tired tears more than anything. We had been walking miles with the kids to get firewood in the little cart. It was hard work. Authentic. Jane was a real niopeer.

And all those visitor nights I couldn't read by kerosene lamp for more than a little while and the days were impossible. I didn't know when I said yes to SCELP that there'd be so little time for my reading. I kept thinking how we were in despair before Mr. Kelvin came and that now we were full of hope. All the early days something about hope was coming to me, an idea without the words. What is it?

10

Irene Lewis

We heard about the SCELP Program from someone in Lamar's office. It seemed like something we should do for the children. Every summer we do something for the children. We've been to Disneyland and Marine World. We've taken camping trips and gone to the Grand Canyon. I don't enjoy those trips much. I don't think Lamar does either. What makes us do this year after year is what we see on TV. All those loving families. I suppose we chose this ranch from the list of possibilities available because of its association in our minds with big, close, warm families. Even while you watch those shows, they gnaw at your heart for what those families have that you yearn for every day and never get. Is it working together? Is it being alone against the elements? Is it need for a simpler life? I never had a passionate marriage with Lamar, but I thought we could have a good life with each other and our boys. We both have interesting and important jobs; the boys cooperate with the housekeeper and are good in school. Our home is orderly and restful. There are no surprises; it's all as dead as the moon.

We read and signed the agreement—participant-visitors, though the boys at fourteen and twelve were not eager for anything more than a tourist vacation. They are quiet boys, careful, serious, even grave. I wonder why. Watching the TV you think of children as brighter, happier, more highly colored than adults, loving change and surprise, optimistic, humorous—they are—we use them as therapists in a sense, like the pets psychiatrists are putting in hospitals and prisons. James and Michael—never Jimmy or Mike, not even to their few friends—were cautious and self-absorbed from their earliest days. They don't like change or drama, they shy away from large groups, learning to be invisible in school and never joining the scouts or the church groups. We thought if they worked with the children of another family—in some vague way—we wanted to hear them talking, laughing, at a chore—we signed up for a week when we were both able to get away—the end of October—and were careful to get the boys' schoolwork so they wouldn't fall behind.

We got the instructions, travel directions, and what to bring. We read accounts of farms and ranches and the material SCELP put out, and we went to Denver and then by car to Bascom. We took the turnoff out of the town and went up Croom Mountain, across the fords and up the narrow rutted road until we came over the top and saw the place. I thought we had made a terrible mistake. The golden Indian summer had passed at the altitude at which we found ourselves—the ground was dry and brown. Still higher, snow was on all the mountains and the warmth of the day, fugitive and dissembling.

I don't know what I expected the Fleuris to be like—TV probably. The man, Akin Fleuri (his own name),

83

seemed a little like a character actor in a show, in which someone else was the lead. His clothes were authentic, but to the 1930s not the 1880s, but they were not remakes, just old. There was something authentic about *him*, though. For one thing, his face. It was windburned and wrinkled; he looked twenty years older than his age. His eyes were blue, old man's eyes, used to looking out great distances. His hands were cut and calloused, scored and marked, grown back and growing back the new skin of old insults. He had come up to the car and introduced himself and his daughter, Kate. He was about to say something more, when she told him there was something he should see to in the barn and he left right away. She told us to park behind the house and she led us in to meet the others. She was charming in her pioneer clothes, a blue dress sprigged with small green and yellow flowers, which went well with her honey-colored hair and delicate features. She took us to the house and we got shown through. It was a hilarious combination of now and then. There was a woodstove in the kitchen, but the kitchen itself was papered with garish modern food. Looking at it, the mother said they were "real proud" of their newsprint wallpaper, but that they would have to replace it as soon as the replica paper was ready, less colorful but more authentic. Still, she said, the method was 1880s. I had to give them that. Mary Beth is a big fat woman, looking like an illustration of pioneer womanhood, but every time she opened her mouth, out came every banality issued between 1950 and 1970. The front room was also papered. It was blinding. "I'll sure be sad to cover over these colors," she said. If the method of wallpapering was 1880s, the message was certainly modern—runners, politicians, Masters and Johnson, I think, looking sternly into the future, all the activity, movement, color, restlessness—it was a reminder of everything we thought we were leaving, an object lesson. Lamar mentioned it, too. The room didn't look much used. We would

84

probably be working elsewhere most of the time, thank heaven.

Lamar and the boys went up to get dressed in their working clothes. Neither of the boys seemed impressed. I don't know what I had been hoping for, but . . . Mary Beth talked about what the week would be like. The men would be checking fence, repairing and redigging post holes for the winter, and we would be doing women's chores, washing and cooking, but in the middle of the week the men would be slaughtering two animals and there would be rendering, sausage making, and getting the tallow ready for soap. I went up to change and check out the rooms. No paper up there, thank God, just white-wash, of which we had to be very careful.

I mentioned the slaughtering to them and to Lamar. I didn't know if the boys should be seeing that—we had signed papers saying that whatever work was to be done at the ranch, we were to be involved in it—I hadn't thought about actually killing . . .

When Lamar came down I told him about the week and saw his face fall. I hate it when he is disappointed. He sulks. I could see his lip coming up the way it does, the way I have learned to hate so much. He said, "Well, that's that, I guess," and flounced out like a teenage girl. Their youngest, Jane, came over to me and took my hand. It seemed patronizing. I felt like slapping the hand away. She's six years old and she was sorry for me.

We went to the corral and the barn and they learned how to harness the horses. It was pleasant in a way— physical but not like the lonely jogging we do, running from nowhere to nowhere. For a moment I saw what this week should be for us, the purpose of it, but Lamar was sulking next to me and the boys were as passive as the little seahorses we had seen last year, bobbing and drifting in the aquarium. I began to measure the time of the week in my mind.

The days passed. Everything passes. The next day

Akin and Robert Luther took Lamar and the boys up to the range and cut out the steer and the calf they wanted to drive down to the corral. They set up the frame from which I guessed the animals would be hung. We got out the supplies and set them up on a sawhorse table outside, and then covered them in case it should frost over during the night.

I found myself liking Mary Beth a little better—she is a complete featherhead and she says whatever comes into her mind, but she's a good-hearted woman and somehow, someway, the work gets done. We all talked a lot. I tried to do my part, to—well, we are paying $250 for this—to cooperate, but I saw I had failed with Lamar and with the boys. Lamar was still sulking and the boys hadn't changed at all. When I'm at work, I forget what my home life is like. Here, it was all home life, where Lamar is palpably silent and the boys, each in his own room, are closed away, doing their homework dutifully, completely, compulsively, and spiritlessly. A big supper. It was pretty bad, heavy and greasy, but the boys and men ate everything. It must have been the work they had been doing. We did the dishes and went to bed to save on kerosene. Our room was bathed in moonlight. Lamar was beside me, sulking in his sleep, the injured, party, even in his dreams.

Another day. We got up, the boys milked the cow and then refused to drink any of the milk. Where did they think milk came from? They said they knew but didn't want to know, that the plastic bottles and waxed cardboard cartons we got at the store hide the awfulness of it—they meant the physicality of it. Louise Fleuri said, "Then, don't let them find out where eggs come from." Michael said, "Aaggghhh." James sniffed and said, "Eggs have shells. The shells keep . . . protect . . ." and then *he* almost turned green. Lamar looked at me across the table for a second and there was a spark of sympathy, fellow feeling, a half-wink, and then the pout came down like a hat that was too big for him, covering his eyes.

Akin showed us how to get the animals ready. The boys put the calf in the barn. They led the steer under the frame and got it down and tied its legs quickly and then hoisted it and cut its throat quickly and the blood spurted into the clean buckets that caught it. I couldn't stop looking, couldn't move or turn away. Something elemental, something as basic as my own breathing had taken me up, eyes, senses—I couldn't even hear what Akin was saying. The steer had given only one great bellow, but the sound—like a last word—hung on the air and drowned out everything. I felt myself standing close, very close, to the body—corpse now—and to Lamar. I heard him breathing hard. The two men, Robert Luther and Akin, stepped in and cut the fleshing cuts in the animal who was now hanging upside down, a Y-cut on top and another, and then they opened the belly. My hands reached out. I heard them telling us what to do, carefully. The Fleuri girls had taken the blood away and put other vessels down to catch the liver and intestines, the tripes and heart and kidneys, as they were cut clear of their connecting tissue. Lamar caught my eye. He was aroused, physically, yes, sexually aroused; I could feel it. His eyes were glowing, his hands trembled. I, too, was feeling something I never felt before, an excitement, a pressure throughout my body as though the blood had begun to beat against the walls of my arteries all over me, swelling them until I thought they would burst. My head was light, almost making me dizzy. My hands trembled, too, and I reached in and caught the steaming organs, glistening and smooth. We were both bloody to the wrists. The blood excited us, caught us. Our hands touched, but we couldn't tell living flesh from the intestine we stripped and lay in the bucket. We worked

87

rhythmically, up and down, like . . . Next to me I heard Lamar breathing in and then he breathed in my ear, "Go in the house."

Mary Beth, Kate, and Louise were cleaning the intestines, getting ready to use them as sausage casing. That had all been explained. The liver, heart, sweetbreads, and the two kidneys in their balls of fat were lying on a tray. The men had moved a stump close to support the head while they cut it off. Lamar mumbled something about taking the tray in and he went and picked it up from the table. The men had gotten to the brain and tongue of the cow and these, too, went on the tray. I followed him, trying not to run or stumble. We went up the back steps and I opened the door for him. He put the tray down on the table and lunged for me. We smelled of elemental things, blood and sweat and the crystalline air, and the air we were breathing, and something else, the smell of one another's desire. My hands were still bloody. We raced to the front room. He was tearing at my clothes and his own. We had always been so dutiful, book-taught, carefully "stimulating" this and that for one another. We are knowledgeable, rational modern people. We do not want shock, surprise, mystery. Mystery is ignorance. Lamar threw me on the floor. He was fully ready; he dived upon me, entered, and we were in one another, riding one another, now slow for me, now fast for him, in a rhythm that built and then—he stopped. "What—" My voice sounded too loud.

"I can't," he said.

"Why not?" I was almost pounding the floor.

"Look," he said. "Them."

They had caught his eye, those professional, parental portraits of Masters and Johnson, peering out of the newspaper picture, stern and vigilant, a new generation of American Gothic.

"Let's turn the other way—we can still—"

"No, it's no good. I know they're there and who they are. Look at them." Thou Shalt. It was worse than Thou Shalt Not. "Oh, God, I'm losing everything."

But he wasn't and we both knew it. There was a calf still to go. Blood and viscera and the thrill and mystery of elemental things, as bare as lightning. Tomorrow, who knew what or how afterward? "We're due back anyway," I said.

He whispered in my ears, "The blood . . ." and I whispered back, "The heart was still beating," and our eyes shone in the talisman-hung room. The next time we wouldn't go there; we would go to some unused outbuilding or upstairs to our bedroom, although I would prefer something more basic, bare, and elemental. We've had enough soft beds, soft music, gentle caresses, and "sensate focus," dutiful as medicine in an old-age home. I want to watch the heart, the still-beating heart . . .

11

Louise

I am trying to figure out to put words to how we changed on SCELP. We are certainly more fragrant in Bascom. In school the teachers ask us special questions and inquire about the visitors we have. We had the Lundgrens and the Lewises and then the Frames and the Beldings. All of them are important somewhere else, but when they come here they don't want to talk about their jobs or describe the lives they have. Mr. Kelvin was wrong when he told Mama we would learn a lot from the visitors about life off the ranch. We are their forgetting, or characters in their dreams. What's it like to be in someone else's dream? It depends who the dreamer is, but there is a way in which you are waiting for them to tell you something, to form you in some way.

So, I think the visitors have changed us more than we have changed them. Time has changed for us. There seems to be more of it, which doesn't make sense when you think about it. Town has speeded up on us; hill has slowed down. When we go to Bascom everyone seems busier, quicker, louder. When I think about this it scares me—what if we go back too far and can't catch up again? What if the world changes in a way we can't understand because we are more and more understanding the older ways? Our words have started to change—all the words for what we do—the skinning and tanning, shoeing, grinding, milling—all the words for those things and the tools we use to do them are older words and have older ideas with them. Our walk has changed; the movements we make are slower and quieter. We seem slower—like people from a 45 r.p.m. record played at 33⅓. Robert Luther and Kate admire their new selves. Robert Luther has begun to wear all his SCELP hats to town. He graduated from high school last year, so he is working at the ranch full-time, but whenever he goes down he stays almost all day, talking to people with his leather vest on and one of his hats.

Robert Luther has eight hats. He seems to become a little different in each one—to me, anyway. I told him that and he laughed. It was between visitors and we were at home—no wood to get, and it was raining and he was trying to sew some broken harness with a special needle and leather thread. "Let me get all your hats," I said, "and name you eight times," and we did.

1. a wide hat, black: Preacher Bob Molasses;

2. a Civil War hat, Rebel, but it is a little too small: Charlie Simple, Private;

3. something called "Pasha" in the catalogue: Mean Eye the Desperado;

4. a cap like a military-school man: Percival Upright, Ensign;

5. a cap supposed to be a student cap: Mean Eye the Convict;

6. a top hat that made him look like a TV wino: Eustace Percival Tosspott;

7. and 8. Two winter caps that sit like muffins: Fargone Fargo, as he drives the team through the blinding snow to get the precious vaccine to the dying baby.

I had forgotten ordinary fun. For months everyone had been planning, working, displaying all that authenticity. We had told stories out on the porch with the Lundgrens and the orientation people, but it wasn't the same as now, alone together in the enclosing rain and no need to be anybody at all. He showed me other hats he wanted in the catalogue. He was smiling. That smile is one of the best things I know. When he's in town he smiles at Mary Blascovic. It's squandered on her, if you ask me. Mary's mirror is only wide enough for one.

All that time after Christmas, One Eye was up seeing Daddy, and if I walked by, I could hear them arguing about more product. One Eye never comes in the house or does things the normal way. He is very proud of his ugliness and tries to keep it perfect. When he argues he turns his burnt side toward the person he is arguing with, to weaken the other person. He wanted Daddy and Robert Luther to be out at the shebang all day. Daddy kept saying that the SCELP stuff had to come first, and when he and Robert Luther could get away between visitors, they would do work at the shebang. Finally, Daddy said if One Eye was so eager, why didn't he come up with a chain saw and cut a little wood for the burner? Daddy told him he could cut down the trees that were already dead. Something made me nervous about having One Eye there, even though it was conversation I wasn't supposed to be hearing. I understood Daddy's reasons.

Over the years there has come to be a big spot around the shebang where the wood has already been cleared, and by now wood was the biggest time-taker Daddy had.

One Eye stamped and cursed and said he wasn't cut out to be a lumberjack. Daddy shrugged. Part of me was proud. The things I saw back last year when One Eye talked to Daddy as if he, not Daddy, owned up here—those things were paid back. Someday I will get the word to describe the good feeling I had, that good paid-back feeling after all that time. I will print that word on a tee shirt and wear it for a year. One Eye finally said that he would come up sometimes and cut wood for the burner.

It was after the Lewises that Mama got the idea of Anglus. Anglus comes from a picture in Kate's Western Civilization textbook. In the picture, some French people are praying out in their field. Mama said that that kind of praying was really authentic for 1880, and not only in France. Our family came from France and *Fleuri* means *flowering* in French. She remembered her grandmother saying that everyone prayed a lot then, house prayers and field prayers and table grace and Sunday prayers. Mama said Anglus was the least we could do.

So we agreed to start it. I guess they really did pray it here, because there's a big bell in the barn that no one ever saw the use of. Mama got Robert Luther to set it up on a hook that was already mounted to the cross-beam of the barn. It fit just right. Every afternoon at six she said she would ring it and we were supposed to stop and spend two minutes praying for the land, the stock, and the weather, which is fair, when you think about it. Then, it's time to come in to supper.

So when new visitors came we told them about the Anglus along with everything else. Some of them said "How charming," and some said "Okay," and some said nothing, but we had Anglus every day right through November, December, and January, except we switched the time to five for the winter.

If you look at that Anglus picture, you'll see that the

man who painted it didn't use many good colors. I thought about the reasons for it, but I could only think of three. Maybe he was too poor to buy good paints. Maybe over there in France the sky looks one color and the ground one color and the people don't have nice clothes to wear. If that's true, no wonder they all came over here. The third reason is that some people don't care about flavors and colors and things like that. Jane copied that picture and put good colors into everything, and I liked her picture better than the Frenchman's—for the color, anyway.

Our visitors talked about colors a lot. When they came in December they missed the big storms that came before and after. The ground was dry and brown and hard. The green of the trees was dusty-looking. The sky had different shades of blue throughout the day, but they were all shades of blue-gray. Subtle, Mrs. Morris said. I learned two words from her: *subtle* (the colors outside) and *variegated* (the parlor wall).

Every morning and evening Robert Luther would go away into the smokehouse, where we kept our modern things, and listen to the weather on the battery radio. That way we could know when storms were coming. The real pioneers must have been surprised and scared a lot of the time, waking up to the awful windstorms and whiteouts and no radio to tell them what was coming.

The Teeters and the Paynes were with us when the second big storm was due to hit. Robert Luther came in from the barn and said, "It feels kind of wet and the milk cows are nervous. I think we ought to rope things." I had to laugh. It was so dry and still you could hear the echoes of the cattle's feet hitting stones on the south pasture. Everyone but the visitors knew that Robert Luther's information came from KOA radio, not the earth, the sky, or the cows, unless they had a cow down at the news microphone reading it all. That's why I laughed and why Kate kicked me in the foot.

So we all went out even though it was dark by then and Daddy had lanterns for everyone, and he got the ropes out and we strung them from the back porch to the barn where there were hooks, and from the barn to the corral, and from the corral to the pasture gate. He showed everyone how to tie himself around the waist and then to tie himself to the guide rope so that he slipped along on it to where he was going and couldn't get lost even if his hand couldn't be on the rope. He made everybody practice. Not one of the visitors understood why. We also hung the rope from the front door to the pump and from the back door to the privy. Then we all went to sleep.

In the morning, there it was, the whiteout: no ground, no sky; you couldn't hear anything but a terrible wind or see anything near or far and the snow did funny things to whatever makes a person think he is walking straight or even walking at all. Everyone praised Robert Luther for being a genius about weather. Everyone said how wonderful it was that a person was so in tune with his environment. I was trying to keep still and Kate was looking daggers at me.

The first test of it all was trying to make it to the privy without getting lost in the storm. Of course, we had gone back to night pots, which Mr. Teeter called "thunder mugs," but even they had to be cleaned and emptied, and you can't just do it out the window in a whiteout because you're liable to wear it all. Everyone took turns tied on and dressed and carrying his mug, and half of us lost the contents anyway, being blown around and clinging to the rope and breaking twelve different paths through the snow because the wind kept changing and the rope had to have some slack to it, and you fell, blown over in the snow, and had to get up again and not forget to use the rope. That's when everyone realized how good it was to be tied on. Mr. Payne and one of the kids lost their directions and came back to the house, thinking it was the privy, and had to start out all over again.

The work of feeding the cattle in the pasture took the whole day and more. Mr. Teeter and Mr. Payne helped Daddy and Robert Luther get the sledge and load it with hay. They had to use the ropes all the time just to get them to the pasture gate without getting lost and freezing two hundred feet from the sledge. We had to get water the same way, tied to the guide rope between the pump and the house: four buckets apiece.

They loved it. It surprised them and scared them and they worked until they could hardly stand up, but they did a lot—double the work Daddy and Robert Luther said they could do alone. They were able to get more bales each time they went out. In the house it was the same. We were even able to get wash water. I always forgot how everything changes in a whiteout, how the silly-looking rope you put up during the season becomes the only idea you have of where home is, how scared you get going outside, that with your luck the rope will break. People thought Daddy's sleeps were his being exhausted from all the work he had done, harnessing the horses and loading the sledge.

When the snow let up, Daddy took the men out on snowshoes to hunt, and they got two deer who were trying to dig for some grass through the snow in the grove that was near the shebang. The men asked Daddy later if shooting deer in February wasn't illegal, and Daddy said, "Ain't I authentic? I didn't go out at night and use no jacklight, the guns is right, the bullets hand-filled, all of it authentic as hell." They field-dressed the deer and brought them home on sleds we have. The men were really enjoying everything, and so were we, telling stories with the visitors and reading to each other. Even milking was easier.

I used to hate the storms because they kept me from school and because when we got caught downtown I had to stay over with Kate's friends, where I am, as Mrs. Gonce, my English teacher, says, uncongenial. Kate still loves it down there. This year we were in town two days in December, one in January, and four in February. We stayed with Mary Bogardus at her house, a huge house, with special bathtubs and everything. Because they have cleaning help, there is very little to do, and Mr. and Mrs. Bogardus are very cheerful and never criticize anyone. That means there's less to talk about and people are less comfortable than they are at home. Saying "How is your hamster?" to your kid means a lot less than "How are the heifers?" The hamsters are pets and the heifers are as serious as survival. They talked a lot about SCELP and asked us lots of questions. Kate loves being from 1880 because it interests people and lets her be popular. Why do I feel wrong about that? Why do I pick at it all the time?

After the storm everything was mud—a sea of it. Everyone was glad for Anglus then because we were falling-down tired from all the cleaning we had to do and the washing outside and all the cooking. It was nice to stop for a minute or two and rest. When the visitors left, they said the experience was a "once in a lifetime one." I said, "So is a prairie fire," and Mr. Teeter laughed and then he reached down and picked me up and said, "Even that is good for people who need to put their efforts to something they can see." I remembered that. I also remembered being picked up and held. It's not only that I'm twelve and too big to have been picked up for a long time, but that I was never cute and sweet like Jane is, so it was, like the lady in my book says, memorable.

As soon as we could make it through the mud, we took the Teeters and the Paynes down to Bascom. We had missed school for three days and Jane, Kate, and I

97

all stayed over for one night to catch up. Now town was interested in our snowed-in days. Suddenly, we were special people instead of lazy no-shows at school. They asked all about how the people had behaved. Had they had cabin fever? Had they been amazed at the whiteout? "Seems it would be tougher on people like that," Mr. Gunderson, the civics teacher, said. "High-powered people." That made me feel a little angry, slow angry in the new slow way we felt things and not knowing why.

New visitors came before the snow had melted off the road. We were going to have visitors steadily between now and the April snows. Mr. Kelvin said that between April 15 and May 30 we would be having only those people who could afford to be caught in a storm and stay over the extra days. They had signed the release that said so. Those were not quite the highest-powered people, I guess.

The Daileys came especially to see the calving. They said they had come to the Croom to let their kids share nature's greatest miracle. They talked about nature's ways and nature this and nature that a lot. Kate asked the kids later and they just shrugged. She found out they had been hoping for Disneyland all along. They missed Tamar and Orpah each giving birth because that happened the day before they came. On modern ranches they make the cows have their calves at a convenient time. The Daileys got Bathsheba.

Daddy saw the first signs and called them to the barn and sent for Robert Luther. Kate and I went, too, because we liked Bathsheba and wanted to see how she did. It was about five in the morning and we had been awake but still sleepy. I feel sort of breakable at that time. It was icy cold, or felt that way, and the fog did things to my hearing. Somehow it made the barn's wood feel rougher to my fingers and my clothes coarser and more scratchy on my body—the morning feeling. We went to where Bathsheba was standing in the barn in the biggest stall. Daddy had put her where there was plenty of room. Mr. Dailey made Daddy move her around so his kids could all see. It was a footling—a bad footling. That's when the calf comes the wrong way first and one foot and leg is out so the bigger part has to come last and sometimes the rest of the calf gets caught on something inside. Daddy stripped in the cold. He was going to try to turn the calf. He went way up inside Bathsheba, and the Dailey kids, who were standing where their parents had pushed them up front, started crying, and the Daileys were saying over and over that they should be quiet and watch because the miracle of birth was wonderful.

The calf was hung up. Daddy couldn't get the other foot down and he couldn't push it back in and hold it up inside Bathsheba while he turned it. Kate told the Dailey kids to come and help her get hot water for Daddy to clean off with after it was over, but the Daileys told their kids to stay right where they were. Kate and I went two or three times and brought the buckets Mama had set on the stove. Every time we came back, things looked worse. Daddy had gotten too tired, and Robert Luther had stripped to the waist in the ice cold to go up inside Bathsheba. Daddy was holding Bathsheba's head and yelling instructions to Robert Luther, and Bathsheba was straining so hard she had shit all over. Bathsheba kept straining and nothing was happening, so finally Daddy decided to pull the calf. Jane came out to call us all in to breakfast and the Daileys shushed her so hard, she went flying out of the barn crying.

I've seen pulling before and I hate it. First, just because it means that something is really wrong and that when it's done it often kills the calf and sometimes the cow also. Sometimes you pull so hard the calf's bones break and there's blood and mess and brokenness. Sometimes you have to cut parts off the calf inside to save the mother. Long ago, I learned that all the things that are wonderful and natural can go wrong and be natural and a nightmare. It would be bad to lose Bathsheba. I hoped they wouldn't have to kill the calf inside her and bring it out in pieces. I was going to tell the Daileys what might happen, but I got started and Kate took over what I was saying and made it something else. I hate that.

As they got the rope and the broom handle, you could see that Mrs. Dailey was furious. They got the rope tied onto the calf's leg, and whenever Bathsheba had a labor pain, they pulled. When I explained it, Mrs. Dailey snapped at me because I called it a labor pain instead of a contraction, which she said was what you're supposed to call it. She was even more furious when Peter, the younger kid, threw up. Then Daddy and Robert Luther felt something give and Daddy went up inside Bathsheba to try to get loose whatever was stuck in there, and Daddy yelled out, "Oh, God, Robert Luther, get Dailey in to help," and he went over asleep in the straw, easy as a cat. Everybody had forgotten how long they had been out there. Robert Luther explained that Daddy was exhausted from all the work of it, and he tried to get Mr. Dailey to help him pull. Mr. Dailey wanted to, but both the kids were throwing up by then and his wife was screaming at him and the cow was bawling and the whole place was noisy as a Pandemonium. I went to get Mama.

We saved Bathsheba but we lost the calf. It was strangled by the cord, and Robert Luther said it was lying so wrong inside her there would have been no way to save it. Daddy woke up and said so later. Where SCELP is smart is that the Daileys had paid already and signed papers saying that there was no guarantee of a wonderful experience of birth, only an authentic one. Still, we had to live with them all the rest of that week. The sight of Bathsheba standing up and eating was not enough to let them know we did what we had to do. Kate tried to talk to Mrs. Dailey, but she only kept on saying it was our fault. "Birth defects are caused by living unnaturally." She said we had used chemical pesticides and polluted the water, that real nature was good until man destroys it. She sounded so sure, I went to Daddy and asked him if we used bad chemicals. Daddy gave me a long stare and then walked away. Later I asked Robert Luther and he said that for years the agriculture people had been after us to start treating our fields, but that we had always been too poor to afford the chemicals or the systems people used to spray them, and that was what kept our yield so low and made us unsuccessful. By the time he said this, the Daileys were gone, still sure we were calf-killing savages.

Anglus worked out very well, even though the Daileys had something against it. Mrs. Dailey said it wasn't right for us to have it because it was religious, which I didn't understand at all. Mama tried to explain that it was authentic and Mrs. Dailey started to argue. Mama shut up like a clam. Later I showed Mrs. Dailey in a history book that the first thing the settlers did in a town after building a saloon was to build a church. They left mad, and we all tried to tell Mama that what they hated was history, not us. We like Anglus so much Mama thought we should read the Bible for a while every Sunday. I like Genesis and Job well enough to stay through Deuteronomy and Numbers. Daddy shrugged and said it was OK with him. Daddy isn't religious, but I think he likes it when we are all together doing something. Reading the Bible is completely A.

The kitchen has become A, too, in the cooking—even though we have not yet gotten the paper for the walls and we still have the *New York Times* pictures of all that special food. We used to buy cookies and candy because

101

Robert Luther loves all that stuff and so does Mama. Say the words *chocolate-covered* and their eyes light up. Now we make all of that, even marshmallows and caramels. We had to stop making the clusters, though. Rice Krispies is NA. That means Not Authentic.

The April snows kept us out of school for a week; they caught us up here. To Kate's disgust. The first week in May, the Barnstables were here with their kids. Two deer came into the yard, looking for fodder, and we needed fodder, too, Daddy said, so he and Robert Luther shot them and slaughtered them, even though they were winter-skinny. Mr. Barnstable said he wondered how we could do it and Daddy said it was 1880 here and there was no regulation of anything in 1880, including popscull. And with that he went out to the barn and came back with two jars of it and put them on the table. Mama yelled, "Product!" and Daddy said, "This stuff was given to me by an old mountain man," and he poured for the men. I thought Mama would have a fit. Before, with no one there, she would have yelled, but when we have visitors, yelling and screaming are NA. I remembered the Daileys and decided that on SCELP, *any* really strong feeling is NA.

The reason Daddy got product and Mama wanted to yell was that it was May and snowing again. In November the snows are wonderful; the cattle are close and the frost falls and you go out after rose-hips, and see your breath smoking; there's an excitement in everything. Your waiting seems part of it all, like having a book before you can read it. In December you want a white Christmas. January's storms throw deep light snows and there's a secret feeling to everything. The ends of the world, the horizons, come very close. The Croom suddenly seems like a hallway, or many hallways that you can move through but are still close around you on all sides. In February and March the snows come hard, like a punishment. They drive away the sun, but the sun comes again and warms things and clears the land and there are warm days like spring and then ice-cold days like someone you love slapping your face. By April you never want to see another snow. But they keep coming, fighting everything, wetter and heavier, with awful winds, and in between there's that NA spring weather, so the trees bud out and the new fruit trees start to leaf and then, like anger, the snow comes in sleet, another and then another. Then you get the May snows and it's then that you get the bad cabin fever because you can't get to school and you can't get the springtime and you have all kinds of equivable thoughts in your head and people yell at each other. Sometimes the snows go on into June, while everyone else in the world is eating strawberries and getting married because it's spring. We were poorest in May. In May the Croom is a Third World nation. Every time there was a thaw we would know One Eye was up cutting wood. Sometimes we would see the truck and sometimes not. He was ashamed. He came in secret and left without coming up to the house.

When the Barnstables and Kirkseys left we had two weeks, and Daddy was up at the shebang almost the whole time. Late in the winter the shebang can be hard to get to. Because of the wood being there, they got another run finished.

Then all of a sudden it was spring and everything melted, ran, bloomed, broke out of the ground. School ended. Mr. Kelvin came up.

We were so proud, we got lined up in front of him, everyone grinning except Daddy. We hadn't seen him for three months and we'd gone back a lot more than he must have imagined or planned for. We were happy and proud at the way we had gotten everyone through the snows and storms and had put up with the Daileys without ever losing our tempers and had done everything as our pioneer heritage said we should. We had summer plans and the Croom looked less and less *like* authentic and more and more real. He looked around. We showed him where things had changed: the barn, the outbuildings, the corral and shed—old tools we were using, ways we were going back to. Robert Luther showed him the wood carving he had learned during the slow times of winter. He had made Jane a little doll dresser with wooden hinges and he had made Kate and me boxes for Christmas, rather than buying presents. Daddy was thinking we could expand the dairy-cow part, get another cow or two, and make cheese, and the whey could fatten the pig. We told him all that and all the rest. Each of us, one after the other, like a report for school. Kate was learning tatting and embroidery so she could do the doilies we had seen in the catalogue. I'm too clumsy to do that, but I got rid of our old plastic jacks and rubber ball and made a set of jacks out of turkey-neck bones and used a string ball. I can churn and make cakes without an electric beater. My buttermilk is wonderful to drink. I wanted to tell him about my sacrifice of reading and thinking—all the time I had given up to become A, pure A, up here, and places in my head gone all spiderwebby from lack of time in them. Robert Luther is going to teach me tanning. Mama made our sunbonnets for summer, and she found that there's a Mexican version of the Japanese lantern that she can make with willow branches.

When we were all through, Mr. Kelvin stood looking at us for a long time from one to the other. We kept waiting for him to smile or jubilate or applaud us. He didn't. Instead, he said, "We've had complaints about this placement. It's got to stop."

12

Kate

We looked at each other. We couldn't believe it. Mr. Kelvin had a paper, a sheaf of papers. He began to go through them one after another, going back and forth as though he couldn't decide which to look at first. "You've gone way over on your requisitions: seeds, machined parts, hardware, hats, shoes, crockery—it was understandable at the start, but your spending has actually *increased*. Here's a bill for three hundred fifty dollars for pump parts—"

"We had to have those special made. The company's been out of business since 1940."

"—and your *food* bills—"

"A lot of those people was on special diets," Mama said, "for their health and their weight and their cholesterol. I never knew about the cholesterol. Mrs. Belding told me it's killin' people like flies and authenticity was the worst thing for cholesterol." She looked so hurt; she had tried so hard.

"We had folks almost every week"—Daddy began to answer for her—"half them people wanted their salad and every kind of fresh food." About the machined parts, he said, the visitors had worked, sure, worked hard, but work doesn't produce metal parts for machines or leather for harness. We were going to need a labstone and bags for grain now we couldn't use the plastic. We had lost some animals we couldn't eat and we would need to replace them and we would need shells for our guns—

"Oh, yes," Mr. Kelvin said, "shells," and he dug around in his papers until he found the one he was looking for. "You've been hunting out of season. *Everything*, people say—quail, grouse, deer, wild turkey—and you've been trapping hand over fist."

"Sure have," Daddy said, "and I want to tell you them authentic rigs'll break your heart. I forgot the cruelty in 'em and the waste, too, because they maim the animal. I ain't seen sufferin' like that for years. I had forgot all of that. I got so I go up twice a day after my lines. They're twice as hard to use, too, the traps. Couldn't we do somethin' cleaner? I wish we didn't have to use 'em, but *authentic* is what we have to be—"

Mr. Kelvin's shouting made us jump, it was so sudden and so surprising. "YOU CANNOT HUNT OR TRAP OUT OF SEASON!! And you certainly cannot use those traps. Are you actually *using* them?"

"Well, we have to, and like I said, they're cruel things—"

"They're to hang on the barn wall, not to use. If you trapped at all, *in season*, you'd have to use the proper equipment."

"But in 1880—"

"You are not in 1880. You can't—it's state law."

"Explain to me what we are—pioneers or not? We took out the plastic, the TV, Band-Aids, Scotch tape, engines, packaged food, all the rest. Out here they've just

106

elected Garfield as President and there are one hundred ninety-four thousand people in the state. Eighteen eighty. We ain't lynched any passin' strangers or shot the three Indians still living in Bascom, but we've got to hunt, trap, slaughter like my granddaddy did then. It was the economy like you said for us to go back to. They couldn't have lived without it. Anyway, this is my land. I own it and pay the taxes on it and am the one who has to beetle-spray it and burn the brush on it and log it careful. The deer are a plague up here. The elk come in hungry, starvin' sometimes. It don't make sense to me, and never did, how a man can't hunt his own acreage."

I had to be proud of Daddy. It was almost the longest talking I'd ever heard him do, certainly the longest to someone not family. I guess he had thought it out, waiting for the time he knew he would have to use it.

Mr. Kelvin went right past it, just like it was the easy talk teachers do in school, or Mama does. He said, "The acreage is yours, Mr. Fleuri, but the deer aren't."

Louise said, "Like the king's deer in England." Louise is a big reader. I wanted to crown her.

"Ain't that why folks left England?" Daddy was almost yelling. "Ain't that why we're American? Free?"

"Let's not get into that," Mr. Kelvin said.

Too bad. Louise, I knew, was hoping they would. Mr. Kelvin wasn't finished. "You people have been holding prayers here. You've been praying."

Mama almost jumped up and down with pride when he said that. Her eyes shone and she gave Mr. Kelvin a big smile. "Oh, yes," she said, "Anglus. We ring the bell—we got the authenticity from the picture—and our name being Fleuri, which is French like Millet, the painter of the picture, and coming over from France when our folks did and all. It works out real well." She was proud and happy, but I could tell she was also out to make up for Daddy's deer.

107

Mr. Kelvin worked that item over for ten minutes. He told her about church and state. SCELP is a state–federally financed project, he said, and that made it impossible for us to pray at all. Surely we knew that sectarian prayers—and any prayer at all is sectarian—were a violation of the First Amendment to the U.S. Constitution. Robert Luther said that the people seemed to like stopping work for a moment to be still just at that time, looking at what they had done before getting ready to come in. I couldn't believe that the Anglus was against the Constitution. Robert Luther said that we don't make people say any special thing, they could just be silent if they wanted to, because the prayers were silent. They could pray or not pray, however they wanted. Mr. Kelvin said, "You might have gotten by with that—might have, I said—but you also say grace; worse than that, you were planning to read the Bible on Sunday—I've heard you were."

Robert Luther said, "Maybe we could read the Bible silently, too."

Mr. Kelvin said that a moment of silence was a foot in the door. "And no silent prayer will be allowed here. None whatever." Mama started to say the "auth—" of *authentic* and Mr. Kelvin almost growled and said, "You can *say* you have faith. You *say* you pray. You can *say* you talk to God three times a day; but you can't let people see you *do* it. And you can't even suggest that *they* do it. You could go to jail for what you've done, hunting out of season, and the program could be closed here and now because of this silly praying. I know you think you're trying for something, and you've done a lot of good, really; some of your visitors have filled out evaluations of their stays here that rated you excellent. But you can't get creative. Check with me first."

He looked around. Our faces must have looked like five empty houses. He realized he had been harsh so he said some other things, gentling things to try to make

108

us feel better. Nice pigpen—nice attention to the details of slaughtering and soap. We couldn't bear to tell him that some of the beef we slaughtered was from illegal longhorns and that without money from our product, the SCELP stipends wouldn't have covered half the extra cost of visitors' diet foods and our machined parts and the vet's visit to Bathsheba and Nebby's shoeing. The vets and hardware store people weren't on SCELP and neither were the supermarket or the shoemaker. They didn't get twenty-five cents an hour anymore for the work they did.

When he left, we were still standing there; no one had moved. Robert Luther said, "I never knew they were giving us grades, like they do in school. It makes me feel—strange." He meant self-conscious.

Mama said, "I wish I was smarter. If I was smarter, I would know . . .!"

Louise said, "But people liked us—everyone except the Daileys. We put up with a lot. Even the Daileys liked *us*—it was nature they didn't like. We should register a countercomplaint. We should evaluate and criticize *them*."

Jane said, "I wish Mr. Kelvin would go back the way he was."

I said, "We never did get that authentic wallpaper for the front room."

Daddy gave a kind of barking laugh and said, "Well, I told you all. I told you all, and now what? What would things have come to if I'd brought up our longhorns, authentic as a dry-gulch lynchin', authentic as tarrin' and featherin', authentic as rabies, anthrax, poverty, and lice. And the popscull. What if we'd told them about that?"

Robert Luther said, "Nothing's changed; we just have to be a little careful about the deer, and we won't call it praying, we'll call it silence. Nothing's changed."

But we all knew it had.

13

Dr. Van Houghton

As a physician, the stresses of my profession necessitate that a certain amount of attention be paid to the leisure activities conducive to physical fitness. Of course, Dorothy and I jog—five kilometers daily for me, three for her—and there's a weekly handball game at the club to which I belong. I play tennis in the summer and we take a ski week in the winter, but one soon realizes that the demands on a physician's time—particularly in my specialty, which is neurosurgery—are far more often intellectual than physical. The body—Dorothy would say—"resents" being neglected and "takes revenge." Dorothy is a woman who has that gender's unfortunate inclination for sloppy, unscientific thinking; her speech is colored, I would say marred, with such inaccuracies, but her point is not without merit. One needs a change, physical challenge. Last year I did some climbing in the West, the year before a white-water trip, but this year a more difficult choice presented itself. The children are growing up—Dorothy had been taking them to her parents' home during my vacations. She pointed out, albeit somewhat melodramatically, that when they were babies we did nothing as a family. During that discussion she also said that having a weekly coffee klatch with physicians' wives is not the same as living with a physician. I'm not apologizing for Dorothy; she's a fine woman. She looks as good at thirty-five as she did at twenty-five. She has many activities besides keeping house, although I am pleased to say that the house is always orderly and well run. I told her that I understood her concern; family problems are endemic in my profession. On the other hand, a program adequate to our daughters' physical capabilities would certainly not be sufficient for mine. It was my colleague, Felix Meyer, who suggested the SCELP Program, and the following week he showed me the brochure he had sent for for his own vacation. I did not feel comfortable with the ethnic placements, but there were three others I thought would fill our needs—a mining camp in California, a seventeenth-century communal farm in Ohio, and a Colorado ranch circa 1880. After some discussion, we elected to go to the ranch for the second week of June. The girls would be out of school and the arrangements could be made far enough in advance to allow me to schedule my surgeries around the dates.

The neurosurgeon's hands are as valuable to him, and, I may add, to society, as those of a world-famous violinist. I included this comment in our preliminary application, and was assured that with the proper gloves, which I could supply, no work would be asked of me that I did not feel desirous of doing, or that would compromise my needs in any way. It is not, of course, a question of personal vanity. I have said this to Dorothy many times when she asked me to assist in various household functions. "Let us hire a man, if need be, to take out the garbage." Over the years it has made her resourceful.

111

She even does small but necessary repairs on our cars.

Having gone through the inquiry and application procedures, and having finally chosen the 1880 Colorado ranch-farm, we were confirmed on our chosen dates and received further instructions, and we arrived in the town of Bascom in good time. It had been an educational trip for the girls, since I had pointed out various things along the way. The town itself is typical Colorado *nouveau riche*—a neo-vulgar alpine architecture competing with a style I can only call Tex-Mex Precious all overlaid on a sleepy ranch town which previously had no pretensions to style at all. The composite is unique. I trust. It gives one cross-cultural indigestion. I pointed this out. Of course, there is also California.

We were met rather effectively, I thought. The young man, Robert Luther Fleuri, came for us in a horse-drawn spring wagon. The car was put in a shed rented by the program in town. We started out. The ride up Croom Mountain was authentic, savage, and to me, exhilarating. I'm not often pleased by things. Too many of us accept less and standards decline. It is the problem with the nation today. At the top of the hill the wagon came over a little rise and there was the ranch—a quite nice 1880s farmhouse—not perfect, of course, but typical and not overdone. I expressed this. The barn, however, was perfect. I asked that we stop and examine it. The family came out to greet us. They were wearing 1880s clothing, but I saw in at least two cases inappropriate shoes.

The rancher, Akin Fleuri, is a somewhat phthisic individual—I would guess long-term but not massive malnutrition in childhood, the typical winter-starve, summer-gorge picture, and at that level, completely, if not satisfyingly, authentic for a rancher-farmer of 1880. Of course, he looks older than his age. His cause of death will probably be pneumonia, secondary to some kind of bronchial trouble. He has the chest. *She* is significantly overweight, if not obese, and probably retarded. I think she would fail a level-of-consciousness examination: orientation as to time and place. She skittered from subject to subject without any consciousness of her discontinuity. Was the West really pioneered by such people? I wonder. Actually, it probably was. Who else would have taken such risks? She will die of chronic heart failure, probably complicated by diabetes.

The girls are charming; the young do not show so clearly what their bodily weaknesses are. The middle one is brainy; it's not a scientific mind, I think, but a literary one. Too bad. The boy—young man, really—seems the one most interested in the SCELP project. As we stood speaking, he told his father about something going on with the cattle, and the older man dropped what he was doing and went off immediately without seeming to notice how strange such behavior was. At other times, the father was cranky. I believe Robert Luther to be quite intelligent. That is surprising. I am not in genetics but one wonders about such phenomena—unless the children were adopted, and if so, one wonders who would have placed them *here*.

The work began. We were to plow and plant a crop of hay and the bulls were to be turned out for breeding. As the day went on, I suggested various improvements in the way the Fleuris did things around the place. I thought I could save time, for example, by plowing from midfield out, and in a circle. Akin said circular plowing didn't come in until the 1940s. He didn't want to try the other way, either. I had good suggestions about the way the dishes were washed and the farm tools stored. I often notice how disorderly most people's thinking is, how random their lives are. They have no logic to the way they organize the simplest of their thoughts and the most ordinary of their activities. I gave up on the wife, Mary Beth, early on. She just stared at me. I could see she

113

didn't understand any of the explanations I gave or the reasons I tried to state as simply as possible. Dorothy tells me that people must find their own rhythms of work and settle into the patterns most comfortable to them. I contend that this is merely an excuse for sloth and self-indulgence. I am constantly improving, changing my surgical procedures to save time and be efficient. It has taken Dorothy years to learn how important optimum functioning is in the home, but she is intelligent and responds well to reason and informed suggestion.

If I have a fault, I suppose, it is impatience. Sometimes I do lose my objectivity and blame others for a lack of intelligence, which they can scarcely help. These people, for example. Eighteen eighty fits them. Their limitations of intelligence and education handicap them less here than they would in modern city life. The young man, however, would make a good general surgeon. He has manual dexterity for small as well as large things, an orderly mind, an attention to detail, and, I believe, perhaps the native intelligence requisite to survive medical school. It is a shame that his level of education will be— is being—lowered by his family.

Akin and I spent the day plowing. I had imagined we'd use the old moldboard—the plow one sees in pictures. Robert Luther told me that the pioneers here found the land too rocky and the soil too shallow and dry to use that sort of plow, so they developed this combing plow. Using a horse and stopping to remove rocks that one hundred years of plowing and planting had not dislodged until now, I found that at the end of the day the muscles of my whole body were quivering with exhaustion. When the bell rang to stop, I was grateful enough for it, glad for the moment's rest before we headed back to the barn and the unharnessing of the horse, which the men did while I went to the place they had set up for a summer bathhouse. There I stood naked, having called Dorothy, and soaped while she climbed a short ladder and emptied buckets of warm water over me. It was wonderful, marvelous, that water. Of course, I realized that it only felt that way because the work had been so long and hard. I had not wished to admit I was tired and had gone on well beyond the time I would ordinarily have stopped. This is courage and will. I am particularly proud of those qualities in my personality. Coupled with intelligence, they have put me high in my profession and have allowed me to enjoy an excellent living and, it occurs to me, have allowed me to follow a horse in the hot sun all day, plowing a rocky field as a form of amusement. For a moment I thought of this ironically, but my colleagues have reason to know that my powers are not simply intellectual, but physical as well. I have not allowed myelf to become flabby or soft mentally or physically. That is the secret.

Elise and Claire helped Dorothy do the woman's work. I had wanted sons; I make no secret of it. I realize that one of the so-called handicaps of being female is social—they are still in the minority in medical school, et cetera, but their dropout rate is still double that of men. They have no will and no perseverance. They have no courage, either. I have always held that women are the intellectual equals of men; their lack is in character and, of course, physical strength. I used to take Dorothy hiking, for example, so I know. We had so many arguments over her inadequacy that we stopped. I know she could never undergo the tension of an eight-hour shift in the operating room.

The girls are, as much as girls can be, healthy and normal physically, but they both have qualities I dislike. They are whiners and tend to pout when they are thwarted. They cry at the drop of a hat. One gets the impression of invalidism, softness, malaise, dampness from them always, a slackness of body and mind. Dorothy says they are timid and should be encouraged. I find them difficult to deal with.

But as the days went on, I noticed the pouting, whiny

115

quality decreasing in them. They stopped complaining; wonder of wonders, they cooperated in the ranch work, and instead of lying in bed in the mornings, which they always do at home to my intense irritation, they were up and dressed early and were ready for the day. And they became quiet. I found this refreshing.

Dorothy also seemed to be receiving benefit from the week. She worked hard helping Mary Beth with the wash, et cetera, and learned to ride well enough to help Robert Luther with the cattle. Before breeding them, our job this week, they had to cut out those cattle they did not want the bulls to get to. They also rode fence and other things around the ranch that took good horsemanship. I hoped, too, to get some riding later during the week. One thing they did before the breeding was to begin was to paint the bulls' hind underquarters with spray paint, so they knew which cows had been successfully mounted. It was a clever idea but of course inauthentic. Robert Luther says that they must have done the painting manually in the 1880s, risking the vicious kicks of their animals. The stock had all been named, and their individual peculiarities were noted—Dorothy became quite the authority on breeding techniques and told us about them, until I had to remind her that it was not fit dinner-table conversation. She actually remonstrated with me, saying that I often discussed harrowing surgical procedures with my colleagues while dining socially with them at the club, et cetera. It was the only time she took exception to one of my statements during the week.

Tuesday was an extraordinary day. Having plowed on Monday, we were to plant, but on Tuesday morning Akin pointed to a minute cloud over their mountain and said that we had better get the haying done. Akin and I worked all morning, spelling one another—one cutting, one binding sheaves. It is hot, dusty work. Flying insects turned up by the cutters get in one's nose and eyes. We worked with wet bandanas over our mouths and noses. Chaff and wheat straw got in everywhere to itch and sting. When it was my time to rest, I looked to see him coming behind me. He had gone to get more binding wire—"hay wire"—and I looked over in the direction in which he had gone to see if he was coming, but the field was empty. Fearing something might have happened to him, I hobbled the horse and left the field, walking over the cut part toward the edge. I found him lying facedown on the edge of the field closest to the barn, his wire beside him.

Of course one immediately thinks of sunstroke or heart attack. It was neither of those things. Although his hat had fallen off, he was alseep, deeply asleep, but he could not be wakened. Of course, without instruments, one cannot diagnose. There was no evidence of the hemiplegia of a stroke, of stroke at all; his respirations were deep but not the Kussmaul respirations of diabetic coma. He had none of the symptoms of insulin shock—the suddenness, the intensity, the otherwise normality—even as I looked at him he entered a normal REM pattern, perhaps a little shorter in duration than—could it be? Could it actually be narcolepsy? I was so excited, I felt like a medical student making his first correct diagnosis from symptoms. From the lower field I could see Robert Luther coming toward us quickly. His head was down so he did not see me, but he would when he looked up. His father was hidden by the drainage bank and its water-holding scrub that bordered the field.

Narcolepsy, I was certain. I had never actually seen it before, and of course it's a brain disorder—a neurological phenomenon—my own specialty. Many, if not most, neurologists and neurosurgeons pass their entire professional lives without seeing this rare disorder. Robert Luther had seen us now—or me—at the edge of the field. I was exhilarated; there were so many questions to ask. When he came up to us his face showed caution—he was wondering what he could tell me. This had undoubtedly happened many times before. What did he know about it, I wondered. He said, "We'd better go back up and finish the field. Dad has these sleeps—he doesn't like it when you come on him. It makes him self-conscious."

It *was* narcolepsy. I was delighted. I felt as though I had discovered something even more rare. "Who has seen your father?"

"Sir?"

"Who has seen him, done the medical workup, what medical center has his records?"

"I don't think anyone has," Robert Luther answered. "No one ever examined him that I know of. Let's go back now and get the horse and plow some more."

I stood up. We put Akin on his side, and Robert Luther moved Akin's hat over his face to shield it from the sun and went back up to where the horse stood, waiting. I asked every question I could think of. I wondered what I would find if I did a neurological exam, an EEG, a tomograph. Robert Luther told me the sleeps were accurately periodic. He did this with reluctance. It is the rarest of all forms of narcolepsy. I could scarcely contain myself. I told him that my interest was purely professional, but it did not seem to make any difference to him. What an opportunity this was for me—the man was a medical virgin, in essence, an unexamined, unevaluated, untreated accurately periodic narcoleptic. No medication, none at all, ever, nothing to alter, contaminate, or modify in any way the course or quality of his condition. Did he dream? Was his post-sleep state like the postictal state of an epileptic? Was there an aura? If so, was it in the sensory area? Visual? Aural? Was the periodicity modified by emotional or psychological or physiological

118

factors? Coffee? Other stimulants or depressants? Did he drink? What was the effect? I had so many questions. What would scans look like? Was the set quality of his sleep a factor of the stable, active life he led? Even as I asked Robert Luther what questions I could, I knew his answers, incomplete and embarrassed, would be the freest and most complete I would get. Akin was not a very verbal man—years of shame, ignorance, and superstition directed against him would surely have rendered him shy and defensive. What I could get would have to be by indirection. I would have to study him, watch him, note his color and his gait before and after his incidents, question the family subtly. Subtlety and indirection are not my strongest points. I have always been direct and even blunt, or so people say. But I had a task and task-oriented perseverance *is* one of my strongest points. I would learn, would know, even though it was a contest between me and my subject. Was this inherited? Perhaps so. If I approached Mary Beth without telling her why—feigning a general interest in the family, I was sure to learn a good deal. With this intellectual stimulus, the vacation took on added zest. There was the physical work as well—I felt a genuine relish for the days ahead.

I continued the reaping with Robert Luther and I watched Akin as he came back toward us. He seemed no different; there was no special grogginess or lack of coordination. On the other hand, he was at the best of times laconic and uncommunicative. There were no signs and he gave voice to no symptoms. My inquiry was not going to be easy.

At dinner I asked Mary Beth about the Fleuri farm, as though about our conditions, ranching, et cetera. This led to talk of the family. It was like blowing up the wall of a dam, asking that woman a question. She talked for an hour straight. I think she told stories Akin didn't know. We all sat there, clinging to the rocks as the flood of words swept over us and on downriver, tearing away trees and houses in its path. I am not usually given to metaphor, but one could hardly restrain one's self through all that monologue. Now and then I would reach out and try to guide the flow, and Dorothy would send a look across the table to me that I could not read.

There were plenty of relatives. *Fleuri* means *flowered*. They certainly did—four brothers, three sisters, cousins by the score. I was in the process of going through them one by one when I realized that had the condition been familial, the shame of it would have been familial also, rather than individual, and that the flavor of Mary Beth's remarks would have been significantly different if that were the case. Robert Luther and Kate—I looked around at the Fleuri children—showed no sign of the defensive diffidence of the marked "special." Mary Beth also was patently proud of them. My interest ended well before the end of her recital.

Looking around the table at the healthy, intelligent products of narcolepsy and retardation, I came upon my own children. Elise and Claire seemed changed in some way, softened, relaxed. The whininess seemed gone; they sat quietly without fidgeting—I hate fidgeting and have always tried to show the girls the wastefulness of such useless motion. There they sat, watching, listening, the lines of discontent that their faces often wore were erased and smoothed as by an invisible hand. They looked now as they did in sleep: tender, receptive, best of all, still.

Dorothy also seemed less troubled. The hard work of the ranch had tired her and she had an attractive bloom from her work of the day. If I had not myself been so tired, I would surely have suggested having intercourse that night.

The next day I was up and out early, watching carefully for Akin's changes. It had not clouded. The weather was hot so Akin decided to go back to the plan of seeding the plowed field. Robert Luther had told me that the sleeps were regular but he would not tell me when they came. I realized I would also have to watch him, and he might, out of misguided loyalty, wish to "protect" his father, although I had tried hard to explain to him that my medical curiosity was scientific interest, the very opposite of common prying. I did the chores with them, we had breakfast, and got ready to do the seeding. In the middle of the morning, Robert Luther came and called his father away. Akin told me to go on walking up the row, dragging the little homemade seeder, a funnel-shaped apparatus with a very small outlet hole that distributed the seeds evenly along the row. I assumed it was another spell. I couldn't run after them, but in five minutes I might amble back on some pretext or other, maybe in time to watch him go down or to time the duration of the sleep or to watch him wake up. I went quickly up the row and then turned and walked as quickly eastward, to a location that would bring me out behind the house. To my surprise, when I came around to the front, I saw Akin and Robert Luther standing with two men in front of the barn. I thought briefly of going back to the field but decided, as long as I was here, to get a hat, which I had neglected to take out with me in the morning. The sun was punishing at this hour.

The talk was spirited. As I passed I heard one of the men say, "It's a Christian's right."

Akin said, "The government is dead set."

"You have a right in your own home, a constitutionally guaranteed right to practice your religion as you see fit." He was a small man, a man Akin's size, but unlike Akin he seemed always in motion, tapping his foot, gesturing with his hand, talking, listening, leaning forward, his face mirroring everything he was hearing and feeling.

Robert Luther saw me and put out a hand, asking

me if I was going to the house, and if so, would I please send out Kate. "Ask *him*," the small man said, gesturing at me. I went on walking.

I had assumed the flap was about the absurd "Anglus" they had. I hadn't the heart to tell them they were pronouncing the word incorrectly. And about the table grace they said. I am not a religious man and I have not raised my children so. A scientist cannot believe in the unproved, but I liked to rest, to mark the day's end. I am not given to exclamations of gratitude, but there is the work-exhausted body and the joy of stopping work, that pouring light, a horse stretching in his harness, tired also. I liked "Anglus." Table grace had given me the chance to look at everyone—why, I do not know. I liked that, too. It was absurd, all of it, seen separately, but it was a part, in some way, of the Fleuri family and what they were trying to do. It fitted them; it belonged. Of course I do not believe in doing or thinking things for no reason. I wonder if aesthetics is sufficient. I went to get the hat and sent Kate and also Mary Beth out to cloud the discussion.

All the remaining time we were there, I tracked Akin and watched him, tracked Robert Luther and watched him. Robert Luther's absences were so skillfully timed that they seemed entirely apart from any plans Akin had. Before I was able to break the "code" of Akin's sleeps, the time was up and we were scheduled to return home. Chances, opportunities, had been dangled before my eyes and at last denied me. I left the Croom in perfect physical condition and profoundly frustrated. The superstition of the ignorant will forever interfere with the rational imperatives of science. Damn them. Damn them all.

14

Dorothy Van Houghton

I had my first affair not because I loved the man, whose name I can't recall, but because I was bitter then and angry and wanted to get back at The Doctor, who is The Doctor everywhere he goes and in everything he does. Richard was never Rick or Dick or Dicky, even when he was a child. The affair went on for a few months until scorn for Richard died in me and self-hate began. My partners after that varied in many ways, but never in one: They all had the same scorn for me that I had for myself. I chose younger men, young and vain, who postured on the beaches and hung around country club pools. Pregnancy and childbirth changed that. The two girls were not what Richard had hoped for, but for me they were a restoration of the joy and self-worth I thought I had lost forever.

When the girls were tiny they were miraculous, and I suppose I did to them what had been done to me—I dressed them too elaborately and worried too much about their hair and petted them in a way that told them that hair and clothes and bodies were all they had.

Picture pretty, picture still. Richard liked that. His disappointment over not having had male children was deep and often expressed. The girls spoiled under our hands, year by year. They got fat and peevish and they glowered under their beauty-shop hairdos. When we had their friends over to play, they were spiritless. It was in the air of the house, the air all of us breathed; the discontent seemed molecular.

But by that time I had begun to have good women friends. We volunteered together, read and worked together; helped one another through a dozen life crises. Self-hate can't stand up to two years of good laughter and lifesaving support. Mine flickered to a sporadic, low-grade fever under the modest, practical matron I had become.

The men I chose changed, too. There were fewer of them and they lasted longer. They got older then, less vain; I chose them discreetly, carefully, from the ashes of bad marriages and the wastelands of divorce. One I got in the early months after the death of his wife. The men knew I was married and that I would stay married; Richard was a habit and the girls too fragile to be reconstituted in a new family. Someday, maybe, someday I hoped someone would come for whom I would be willing to brave Richard's killing scorn. For now it was enough to cut my life into portions: a satisfying and nurturing portion of my friendships, the comforting one of lovers— one for the past two years—and the arid and mechanical portion that is life with my husband, including the frustrating and sorrowful one of my children.

Not all of the "home" part of my life is grim. I take a certain pride in what I do as a homemaker. The casual visitor or visiting relative says to himself, "Good wife, good mother," and goes away cheered somehow. For me it's a declaration of dignity, a secret kept in dignity. My home.

Of course, the worst time for me is the week-long family vacation Richard insists on twice each year. I have never been able to ascertain whether or not he enjoys these "holidays." He does them the way he does most things, with a dry, humorless rationality, the way people take vitamins or go on special regimens of diet or purgation. We've been to Yellowstone, hiking, ski weekends at Tahoe, and one of those Outward Bound things, where they teach you how to rappel off cliffs. "Medicine" is the curse of the medical profession. Four doctors' wives I know are addicted to drugs. I take Valium only during those weeks, one winter, one summer, when "togetherness" forces us to endure more of one another than anyone wants. Richard goes off by himself on a second week each season and we all breathe easier then.

So I was well weighted with Valium when we went up Croom Mountain and met the nineteenth-century head-on, the rancher and his family with whom we were to live, and whose lives, I thought as I got out of the car at the top of the hill, we were to sour for a week.

The family was pleasant. I liked Mrs. Fleuri on sight because she was big and motherly and dithering and would drive Richard crazy, given half a chance. She was as dumpy as I am carefully slim and modern-woman-boyish. She has two teeth missing on the right side, but she smiled easily—she didn't seem to care that it gave her a slightly jack-o'-lantern look, not menacing, but funny. The girls were lovely. There was a young man, Robert Luther, and the father, who looked like something carved, under a battered hat.

The pleasant surprises continued. The world of nine-teenth-century Croom Ranch was divided into men's and women's arenas of work for most of the day. The men were plowing, planting, cutting hay; the women would cook and wash and clean and bake; and the kids would be taught milking, herding, and caring for the animals during this less difficult time of the year. If Richard was his usual critical and perfectionist self, I wouldn't have to see it. He would be learning many new skills, while I knew much of what I had to do, although in a different form. I loved having the company of other women while I worked. Kate, the eldest daughter, did a lot of the ranch work but also helped in the house and with the washing. In the beginning, my own dour girls showed no lightening. We got settled and then I began work, laughing and talking, telling stories, singing old songs. We put up the "authentic" paper that had just come to replace what they had on their parlor walls. Too bad; I had liked what they had there infinitely better, although no one could stay in the room for more than five minutes. The "authentic" paper was in keeping, and we had to put on three layers of it to cover the old. The room lost personality; all the women agreed, but there it was, authentic. I stopped my Valium the first morning I was there.

Every now and then I would see the young man, Robert Luther, looking at me. He tried to do it subtly but his glance would stay a moment too long. I knew he admired my figure—and that he sympathized with me because of Richard. He got clumsy and self-conscious when he thought I was watching him, and he seemed unable to talk to me directly at all. I thought it moving and sweet. He is just beginning.

On Monday, Elise and Claire took their wood wagon and walked to a place where Kate said there were wild strawberries growing. They came back barely in time for dinner, tired and sun-warmed, and—wonder of wonders—no longer whining or complaining. Across the dinner table Richard was holding forth about how the Fleuris could farm more efficiently—this from a man who had been on the place for somewhere under thirty-six hours and who hadn't worked a plow before this morning. The next day I saw even more of a change in the girls, and a change beginning in Richard, a softening, I thought. He no longer favored everyone with his opinions on everything. I had been out to the pasture with Kate when she drove the two bulls from a different field into the one where the cows were, for mating. They had sprayed the bulls' hind underquarters with colors so they could tell later which bull had mounted which heifer. We didn't stay to watch—Kate said it made the animals nervous. I thought this showed a nice sense of delicacy—we could have hidden behind a rock and seen it. We walked away, having come up with Kate on the single horse—the other two were readied for the hay wagon. Robert Luther came out of the woods at a run and commandeered Achsa, the horse, telling Kate he had to get to Akin about something. We walked back, and on the way Kate showed me how to identify some of the mountain flowers we were passing. I began to think about innocence—the flowers, probably, and Kate's fresh, young womanhood. It made me think of Robert Luther, of virginity. I thought he might be a virgin—I don't mean the pawing around they do younger and younger these days in the backs of old cars. . . . Somewhere on that trip back I decided that if I got the chance I would teach Robert Luther how to make love.

On the face of it, it seemed impossible. Much of my day was spent with women's work—in its natural round, there was little chance to get him to myself. He was shy and, when I watched him closer, I was sure I had been right, a virgin. I didn't want anything furtive, quick, or crude. I wanted something lovely, a dalliance. I began to watch for moments, choices I could make. That evening, Robert Luther told us at the table that he needed to inspect the cows the next morning while Akin and Richard finished plowing and began seeding in another

127

field. I asked if I could go up and help inspect the cows I had helped to mark. The request was natural. I hoped Elise and Claire would want to do something else. They did. I went out to the night chores with Richard and Robert Luther, learning how to put the ranch to bed. Richard was quiet for once. He seemed either tired or preoccupied, and he had amazed me at dinner by drawing out Mary Beth and Akin on family history, to their great delight. I thought it was a wonderfully gallant thing to do and not his style at all. Going out to the barn in the lantern light I looked for a chance to tell him so, but none came. We saw that the horses had enough grain and that their stalls were secured. Robert Luther said that they had once lost a good horse when it had gotten out one night and into a grain bin that had also been left open. The horse had eaten itself to death, which horses will do with grain. I was amazed. I had thought that we were the only animals who lived beyond our means, in food and sex and money, who slept too long, craved comfort and ease too much. I said this and heard Robert Luther laugh in the darkness, a laugh half high, half low, a faint memory of his childish voice, breaking in the middle. I wondered why neither of my little girls seemed to have developed what stupid people call a crush on him, one of those beautiful-aching, desperate-yearning, long, lonesome teenage pains so wrongly called puppy love. It is love, a kind of love that will not come again. It should never be trivialized or ridiculed. If Robert Luther felt something like that for me, I would see it gratified without any cruel wit at his expense. I hoped Elise and Claire could—would—feel as deeply someday as I had about the boys I still remembered. Thinking these things, I followed in the soft light of the lantern Robert Luther held, seeing the shine in the eyes of the silent animals one by one, and hearing them breathe in the darkness outside the small ring of light. Somehow the mystery of such things is made greater by the meta-

128

phor—a tiny warm glow hung in a vast darkness. When we went out, Robert Luther turned the lantern down so we could see the stars. I looked up, amazed. I had forgotten or never known how many there were, how close and intimate they could seem. There were so many that they gave their own light to walk by, even though there was no moon—light in the absence of light, intimate as life was here, they seemed to visit the earth with kindness. I whispered "My God!" and touched Robert Luther's back in the darkness. I did it because, looking up, I had lost my balance a little. Robert Luther, trembling, let me orient myself by holding on to him, but he did not touch me or put his arm out for me. I soon got my bearings and we went to the corral and the soddy storage house to see that its door was closed, checked the pasture gate, and came back to the house, leaving the night in its splendor behind us. I knew also that he was physically conscious of me walking behind him, that he was aware, continually, overwhelmingly, of my presence, coming or going, that I disturbed him. I knew this by the shiver he had given under my touch, a flinch, light as it was definite, but not a flinch of surprise—he had flinched almost before my touch—because he had awaited it in an exquisite consciousness I remembered from my youth.

It would be unfair to say that Richard is not a good lover, but he is not an affectionate man. It would be unfair to say that I am undervalued by my recent lovers, that I am starving for affection; I am not a cruising shark, rapt and hungry for anything warm in the waters where I hunt. But in my ordinary life I am serious enough. This once I want to do more than be passive, setting my light against the darkness and hoping that if there is time and opportunity he will come to it.

Wednesday morning I nearly changed my mind. Robert Luther was busy with all the work of an 1880s farm-ranch. Tuesday I had followed him up to the pasture with Kate to spray the cattle for mites, and we talked, but he had been preoccupied with something and had left us abruptly to go to his father in the field where he was with Richard. They were to come up later to cut the impregnated heifers out of the herd and allow the others their chance. Then he had disappeared for three hours or so and we did not see him until early afternoon. I began to think that for all my planning and his desire, the logistics of ranch life would keep us from one another. It gave me a new insight into American Victorian sexual mores of the early West.

Mary Beth said she needed my help getting a wash out in the morning. When she had been to town she had gotten two big flats of strawberry plants and a flat of strawberries, and she asked if the girls and I would like to plant them. We could make jelly. The girls surprised me by asking if they could get more wood in the little wagon. Robert Luther said he needed one of us for work up in the pasture, riding fences. Then, without my having to volunteer, Mary Beth said that I had probably made enough preserves in my life and that I should go with Robert Luther. Akin had barn work and said that if he needed help he could call one of the girls. I found myself riding Achsa next to Robert Luther on Balthazar. It gave me a special pleasure that this had come without my planning. We rode companionably through the pasture gate, the whole afternoon before us. Though he was shy at first, once alone I found him easy to open up. He wanted to talk about himself, about the way they had all changed on the program, about what I corrected for him as Angelus, about his secret dream, college, in a few years when Kate and the others had grown enough to take his place. He had a tremendous loyalty to his family, which I found endearing, and he wondered aloud if college was not a silly dream when what they were doing required his presence and was the only hope for the ranch. I was surprised at some of this and asked a few questions. He answered them; yes, he had had two very fine teachers in his high school. "I think you should talk to them, or to the school counselor, if he is any good," I suggested.

"I—I haven't talked to anyone," he said. It sounded forlorn under the carefully dented stovepipe hat.

"Why not?"

"When you say a thing, it makes it real in a way."

"When you've made it real you can choose to do it or not to do it."

"There are other things—things that happen around here that I—that we— You should have worn a hat," he said. "The sun's hot. You could get sick."

He had come away from his secrets, which he probably saw as being seditious—treason against a family he loved and disloyalty to a plan he had helped convince them of. In trying to put that idea away, he had come upon me, sitting beside him so close that our stirrups sometimes struck one another. I was on his right. "What are we up here to do?" I asked.

"Ride fence," he said. "I could have done it alone, but . . ."

I said, "I'm glad you didn't."

Up and up we rode. Over the first fold of Croom Hill, the meadow lies wide open, receiving the whole sky. The horizons are forever and are only limited, on all sides, by the curvature of the earth. If I looked out too much I would surely fall into the sky. I looked at the ground, growing its coarse green cover and here and there a purple or yellow sprinkle of some wildflower. I looked at Robert Luther. He was suffering. I could see it. Now and then his hand trembled on the rein. He covered it with his free hand. We really might not get another chance. I said, "Why not rest awhile now and ride fence later?"

He only nodded and looked away. I dismounted but

he was in no condition to try to get off a horse. I looked away and busied myself tying up by the trail. We were near the top of the pasture. The fence bordered the woods that began the north face downward. When Robert Luther was able to get down and tie his horse, I took him by the hand and we walked for a short distance, looking for an easy place to get through, which we soon found.

The woods were cool after the open pasture. I began talking slowly about morality, telling him that what we wanted to do wouldn't hurt anyone, not because it was unimportant but because we understood its place in our lives. Et cetera. Et cetera. The words sounded strange to me, sophomoric, almost ridiculously so. I had never had to say any of them before. Then I stopped him and turned to him, brought his head down between my hands, and kissed him, first lightly on his lips and then, when he opened his mouth to protest, deeply. I had to teach him not to devour, not to kiss as though it was combat. I had forgotten the "passionate" approach the young men used in the backs of all those secondhand cars all those years ago.

It wasn't particularly pleasant. I had to teach him how to embrace, how to enter, how not to ride. I said once, "Make love, not war," and had to laugh to myself because he didn't get the allusion—he's too young. We finished very quickly, but the young male's capacity is, besides his beauty, one of his few sexual advantages. The second time was better, the third, better still—almost good enough.

I was tired by then. We had gradually gotten undressed. We started to put our clothes on again. I saw guilt beginning in the way he turned away. I allowed myself to get a little angry. "I won't be part of your thinking that this is dirty or sinful!" I told him we were good people, which he felt innately to be true. He was probably thinking about Richard, about how he would have to face

132

him this evening, work alongside him, to see and be with him for the rest of the week, knowing this part of Richard's intimate life. I said, "The marriage is not your problem; it's ours." In fact, I used every modern sophistry of the sexual revolution, none of which he had ever heard. Their originality for him and the fact that he wanted to believe them gave a sparkling new-coined brilliance to all of those old pennies that almost amounted to revaluation. His face eased.

I'm sounding like Richard now, and I shouldn't. I'm not as modern or liberated as I sound—as I want to be— and guilt makes me brittle sometimes. We got back on our horses and went on with our job checking fences. I made him talk again. He was an intelligent young man who was in a serious quandary. The SCELP Program was moving them all back in time and he saw it as the salvation of his family and the ranch and the celebration of a way of life he deeply admired. But . . . I asked him what was behind the "but." Did he have a feeling of a special calling, or was it just the call of the world outside, something bigger and more exciting than riding fence and managing a therapeutic experience for tired technocrats? "I don't know," he said, and as he looked at me in his confusion, open, unveiled, a little frightened, I felt more deeply for him than I had for anyone in a long time. "I'd like to wait—four years, maybe five," he said, "but could I get into college then? Wouldn't it be too late?" I told him that people today are going to college for the first time at fifty. "*Really*?" "See your teachers," I told him. We rode on.

Suddenly, he stopped. He stood up in his stirrups and said, "Oh, damn!" and then he sat back down, looked at me, and said—sadly, I thought—"Can you keep a secret?"

I almost laughed and he got the thought, but didn't smile. "Yes," I said, trying to look serious, "I can."

He nodded once, quietly, acceptance without cynicism. I wondered how he did that. Then he nodded and said, "Come on."

We moved up then over to where the woods began, keeping to the edge between the softer hill of the pasture and the steeper, craggier slope of the woods. Scattered over the pasture was a group of feeding animals, a strange, a fearsome, a beautiful kind of animal, smaller than the large ones I had seen on the nearer pasture. These animals were—the horns—they had a primeval look. "Are those what they call longhorns? They're *beautiful!*"

He laughed. "Yes, they're longhorns, but they're not supposed to be here. Someone left the two gates open, or else there's fence down between here and where they're supposed to pasture. They've got to be rounded up and put back, and all the fence between here and there checked. I can't do it alone and you don't know how. We'll need Kate and Dad. I want you to go back the way we've come. Follow the hill, keeping pasture on your left, all the way over until you come to the creek. Cross it and you'll see a trail. Take that through the woods until you see the barn on your left; it'll lead you right home. Don't race, but don't stop, either. Tell Dad in private what happened and go get Kate and send her out on the horse you're riding. Then you'll need to stay with your family and see they don't come back this way. The longhorns are a secret—it's all I can say. I hate to"—he looked away—"I hate to have this—and make you . . ."

I turned Achsa and headed home. Robert Luther had been tactful to give me the instructions as though I, not she, were in command. Achsa did it all and faster than I wanted her to. I saw Kate at the house and called on her to come running. Luckily no one was there. I told her as well as I could that Robert Luther wanted her and described where he was. I said longhorns, and she did a startled double-take and then understood. She said she would take Achsa back up and tell Akin on the way.

"He's with Richard."

"I know. I'll have to get around that."

"Let me come with you. I'll get Richard's attention and help him get the harrow out of the field for the day." I felt a certain sympathy for Richard then. They were having to circumvent him the way I did, probably the way the nurses in the hospital did.

Kate nodded, then looked at me and said, "Yes, thanks." I knew that she had seen me looking now and then at Robert Luther, and Robert Luther looking quite a lot at me. She was having to be grateful when she didn't want to.

Perhaps it was tiredness or the heat of the afternoon, but Richard was a lot less supercilious, letting me help him move the harrow and seeder and pull them out of the field. At the barn we tried to clean the plow and get it ready to be put away as best we could. Kate had told Akin that the herd had come through the fence somewhere. She hadn't said which herd. I told Richard they might be awhile rounding it up. Richard was exhausted, I could see. Sweat had come and dried on him many times during the day and he seemed to be working for more than his own fitness. It made me a little proud. He asked about the girls. "Still doing the wood-wagon work," I said. "They didn't come back for lunch." He said he was happy about that. They are whiny girls. They have never stuck with anything, "but they are now," I said.

"Yes," he said with an incredulous nod, "they are now. If only I could get Fleuri to tell me—to let me—"

"Let you what?"

"Nothing," he said, and to my surprise he walked over to the shady side of the barn and sat down with his back against the wall. In a moment he had fallen fast asleep.

I thought about Richard and about the girls pulling that wood wagon all that way for days. Family pride—they get it from both sides. Yet the four of us, our family, were together at last, sharing the work of a day at least some of the time. We were, at that moment, something like what families are supposed to be.

I went to the house and told Mary Beth that Kate, Robert Luther, and Akin had taken the three horses to the upland pasture. For a while she dithered, but I couldn't tell her I knew any more. I, too, was hot and tired and headachy from too much lovemaking.

After Angelus, everyone drifted in. Robert Luther looked at me and nodded over the heads of Richard and the girls. They were limp with exhaustion, almost too tired to eat. Richard and Akin did the evening chores and had dinner, and we all went to bed as soon as it was dark.

The place and the opportunity were against Robert Luther and me, but we were alone three more times to make love. I will never know how much he learned, how much he used, whether he realized his dream of college or his hopes for his family, but the thing I took away from the Croom Mountain had little to do with him. The moments I remembered most keenly were those of the Angelus, standing up from the washing or the gardening or the haying in the silence after the bell's sound stopped. I remember my prayers for forgiveness that were touched with gratitude for the long honey-yellow light of late day, the sight of the distant trees pooling themselves to green-black shadows. Everything goes still then; there's no sound, but suddenly a bird up from foraging in a new-grown field will shoot head high, break open sudden wings to hang exultant for a second in the splendid light, then tear away singing. I'll remember that longer than my infidelities, longer than Robert Luther or the cry of our bodies pressed together.

15

Kate

Neither of their kids wanted to be here. Elise, the older one, had told that to Louise and Jane on the first afternoon. It had made Jane cry. Jane wants to love the visitors, all of them. She makes paper dolls of each of them, drawing their faces and bodies as realistically as she can, and she puts them into families and plays with them for hours. Other kids hadn't wanted to be here— the Van Houghton kids made it personal. Jane has never been hated before; she's too young to take it and hate back with it. Like the taste of popscull, it's a flavor that people have to come to after practice. Its first taste burns like wood-ash lye. It was the Croom they didn't like, but they made Jane suffer and Louise got angry and I came to hate them for it.

They seemed to want that hate, Elise and Claire. From the first hours they were here they taunted us just out of earshot of their parents, baiting us to dare to be cruel in return, making us know that we couldn't—because we were servants, and servants can't.

They weren't like the Dailey kids, who had just wanted to be left alone. Most of the haters I know are poor or ugly and are angry about that; I couldn't think of the reasons these ordinary kids should have so much of it. When their parents were listening, they were pouting or silent, not giving a thing. When their parents were gone or lost in the noise of work, or talking to one another, they tore away the lie that we were independent, that they were visitors, guests. "If you want to keep this place going, you'll . . ." all the time. I had to ask Mama to help save Jane, that when there was work to do, she should send Jane someplace, away from them. I didn't give the details, but Mama screwed up her face and said, "That whole bunch makes me feel like I've got hair growin' out my nose and ears. The Mrs. is nice, poor thing. Otherwise, I'd give 'em all a hotfoot and send 'em all down mountain with it."

I was surprised. Mama has always flown over things, laughing them to sleep or changing them into dreams. Once a visitor told her she overcooked everything and she laughed and said, "Ain't it authentic, though—Lord, our family's been doing that for generations!"

That was how we came to send them out wood gathering with Louise on their first morning here. I told Louise that if they were too hard on her she should lead them to a place where they could see the ranch from the road and leave them. "That Elise is fourteen; she's old enough to be by herself. Warn her what to look out for."

"Mountain lions and rattlesnakes," Louise said, "three and one-half minutes to a horrible death—just in sight of help—your throat is choked with blood so you can't cry out." Louise enjoys being hated because of the drama of it.

I felt guilty telling Louise that she could leave the Van Houghton girls, but it was servant's revenge, after all. We worked through the day without seeing them, and the Van Houghton grown-ups were the only ones who didn't know and so were easy in their minds about them. Louise had come back an hour after going out. When they didn't come home for lunch, Mama sent Louise back with sandwiches, which Louise swore she delivered. I don't think she did; I think she left them on a tree stump near the road. She and Jane spent the rest of the day getting brush in the second wood wagon.

So it was a relief when the two of them came in after Angelus, pulling their wagon with a token load of light kindling. They didn't say anything, but they seldom did when they were with their parents. I thought I saw something less sour in their looks. Maybe it was the day alone with only each other to be mean to.

The next morning we made soap. Dorothy, Robert Luther, and I went to paint the bulls. In the afternoon, the girls, including Jane, went back with the wood wagons. I was expecting to hear protests from Elise and Claire, but they surprised me by taking their wagon with no complaints. I was still talking to Louise and Jane while the Van Houghton girls were walking up the road. "Stay in sight of them," I said. "But not in sound," Louise added. "Okay, not in sound." I couldn't blame her. We needed the wood.

With every day that passed, we were more aware that three horses were not enough for the work we had to do, four of us and our visitors. Most of the time, one or the other of the horses was having to be ridden double and, as Jane said, none of the horses had signed up on SCELP but they were all on it and worked harder than we did. It was trouble with the horses, not trouble with the visitors, that we talked about most when we were together. Mr. Kelvin had told us absolutely not to make any more requests before the new fiscal year, but this problem was so obvious I thought we should try one more time. I was working to drum up support for a good argument on the Encumber forms. Robert Luther agreed at last, and Daddy said disgustedly that this seemed to be Kelvin's ranch now and Kelvin would have to be shown the need for more horses. I hadn't known that he felt the servant's harness on his shoulders, too.

I was thinking how to express the whole thing on the paper, how to number the boxes with the coded computer numbers that showed purpose and use. Mr. Kelvin was due to come up in a week or so, and I wanted all of us to be ready for him, but the Van Houghtons had put everyone in a bad mood and no one answered anyone else with an encouraging thought. We were all just trying to survive them.

On the ride up to the high pasture Dorothy and I talked about nothing in particular. We were riding double on Achsa. I noticed that she and Robert Luther did not talk to one another at all. He was almost dumb with her. I had to be the one to explain how we were going to mark the bulls. The afternoon sun was hot and in the open we were even hotter, but we got the marking done, though not in the 1880s way, which was dangerous, but in the 1980s way, spray-painting them. Then we turned them out to breed. We had just finished with Omri and had driven him through the gate where the cows were waiting, when Robert Luther came running to me and said, "Get off Achsa—she's faster than Balthazar. I forgot about Dad!" I slid off, and Dorothy and I rode home slowly on Balthazar, leaving it to me to make up an excuse. I was getting good at them.

We came over the hill within sight of the house and barn just at Angelus time. Everything in our little cup of valley looked glowing and good. Mama was in the barnyard ringing the bell. I saw Louise and Jane coming up the road with a wagon full of brush. It was easy to see them now that the hay had been cut off the home field, and there at the edge of the woods I saw something bright and made out the second wagon. Elise and Claire had stopped for the bell. Everything was beautiful in that moment; perfect peace, and 1880. Dorothy, who was riding behind me, breathed out, letting her troubles go. The only sounds had been those of birds feeding in the new-cut field. The bell-beat scattered them, and their wings between the beats sounded like applause. We all stopped for the bell to echo past where we stood, lifted up and away from us into the places of later light. That was the minute I thought I saw a small miracle.

The second wagon began to move. It had not been loaded high or carefully tied; I could see it was side-heavy even from where I stood, and it began to overtake the first wagon. Both girls were pulling. As we watched, it came up side by side to Louise and Jane's wagon, and both then went along together. I half-expected the first wagon to pull away, but it didn't. The four girls might even be laughing or talking. I thought, Could it be? Could it really be true what Mr. Kelvin said about our ranch being able to heal people? Could all this light and bird-sound and work and us—could being with people who lived in another century really heal what was bothering modern people? There came the wagons, companionable as old dogs, and there were the girls going toward home, and now and then we got the sound of squeak in one of their wheels on the evening up-slope breeze and an echo, I was almost sure, of a scrap of laughter. It was like a hand smoothing something deep inside me. Dorothy touched my arm and I turned and she said, "Let's go down to them."

At the barn we saw the doctor, who had come in with Daddy. He was filthy and sweating and it made me glad to see him with hay in his hair and know that his knees were hurting and his shoulders were quivering and muscle-bound. I have done some of that harrow plowing,

141

and they had been at it all day. Dorothy went over to him and I went to meet the girls on the road.

Closer, the scene didn't look so beautiful as it had from the hill. Jane and Louise looked guilty and the Van Houghton girls half-dead. Their faces were streaked with dirt. They had been stopped on the road with exhaustion and were only now coming with their badly piled wood to the house. When I talked to Elise she only stared back at me. Claire had been crying. Their faces were red and very hot-looking. "These girls got too much sun," I said. Jane's eyes started to tear up. Louise said, "We lost them. We thought they were lost in the woods. We called and called. We didn't see them all day."

"I told you to stay in sight of them, but I guess it's all right. They probably fell asleep in the sun. Take them under the pump and I'll run it for you."

Although the pump water was icy, the girls were so hot and tired that they barely protested. I was ready with all kinds of answers and excuses because I was sure they were going to accuse us of letting them get lost in the woods all day and only finding their way by the Angelus bell. I was wrong. They sat at the dinner table without a word, mute with sun and exhaustion. All the Van Houghtons were quiet. It was a wonderful meal.

But afterwards, Robert Luther signaled me to go out to the barn with him. Elise and Claire had fallen asleep at the table, and before we went out we led them up to their beds. When we were on the stairs, he whispered to me over their heads, "Van Houghton knows about Dad's sleeps." My heart sank. After we saw the girls to their room, we went back down the stairs and outside.

I love summer light with its long shadows. From the barn we could see back to the house where Daddy and the doctor were out on the porch, sitting out there after dinner with Jane. "I should be helping with the dishes," I said. "Everyone is tired out."

142

"Van Houghton asked all kinds of questions." Robert Luther had contained himself all afternoon and couldn't have kept still another minute. "He told me Dad's sleeps are some kind of special, rare condition. He was eager as a ferret. He's probably pumping Dad now for all kinds of information."

"Daddy won't say anything; you know that. And the doctor can't *prove* anything. As far as he knows, they're what we say they are—sleeps. You didn't tell him about the timing of them, did you?"

"Of course not . . ."

"Then he doesn't know when they come, or how long they go on."

"No, I guess not." Robert Luther was relieved. He saw what I was getting at. "You think we can just keep doing what we've been doing—not let him see any more? Dummy up?"

"That's all we can do—play the role."

"Disappear," he said, in a strange way, "into the role." I nodded, and then he grinned at me and said, "Where did you get so smart?"

"Croom Rube School." We laughed. "It's always 1880 there." But I could see that he was sad, and for reasons beyond the doctor and his questions.

The next day was hot also, and I was surprised when the two Van Houghton girls said they would go out for wood again and went to their wagon as naturally as though they knew and cared how much we needed brush for our fires. When I went to tell them good-bye and to be careful, they were already moving up the road and I was too relieved to stop to wonder at it. Dorothy and I were to work helping Mama get a wash out. It was going to be a scorching day. Dorothy was good at pitching in. She worked with us as though it were crisp October, hauling and heating water, and after lunch she went up to ride fence with Robert Luther. Part of the clothes-washing time I spent dreaming of faraway things, a nicer family to be visiting us, a nice boy, maybe, who would look at me the way Robert Luther seemed to be looking at Dorothy, but without the shyness. Daddy's sleep was meant to come at eleven-forty-five. I got them walking in for lunch and gave Daddy a line about the hay in the haymow being wet. He sent the doctor on a goose chase and went over on a bale in the barn. The next sleep was at six-thirty in the evening, and that one would not be easy. They would probably be cleaning up after work. I thought about sending Dorothy to get the doctor for a shower right after Angelus. The pressure of his knowing about the sleeps, of his wanting to see Daddy sleeping, made me more anxious than ever that he should not see any more; he would be trying to get past all the fences we were making to keep him out of that private part of our lives. It was a drone in my mind all morning as I washed and rinsed and wrung, and while I hung clothes in the hot, white air of afternoon. Daddy's secret had come to mean more than keeping some pushy doctor from looking at Daddy like a case; it had come to stand for what we had a right to see as our own, private, unshared: longhorn authentic, not front-porch authentic. Dorothy had spent some of the morning telling Mama about her trip to Paris. Mama told Dorothy that Daddy's people had come from France in 1840. Mama is the only person I know who can say "Paris, France," with all the wonder there is and none of the envy.

The Van Houghton girls didn't come in for lunch, but no one worried. Mama said they'd be back later and she'd see they got something to eat. Elise was fourteen, after all. They were probably eating strawberries. We'd shown them how to find them on their first day. Dorothy left with Robert Luther. Mama and I hung wash. I didn't have the heart to tell her about the doctor, and something was nagging me about Elise and Claire going off again this morning. . . .

144

We had gotten everything done and emptied the boiler and rinse water and turned the wash-boilers upside down on the stands Robert Luther had made for them. I was ready for a rest, and we were turning for the house and porch when Dorothy came riding up, waving and calling to me, and when I went to her she jumped off Achsa and told me about the longhorns. I rode back quickly and told Daddy to take Nebby, leaving the doctor and Dorothy to pull the harrow and seeder out of the field.

By the time we had rounded up the longhorns and driven them back through the broken fence and Robert Luther had done temporary repair, it was almost time for Angelus. Robert Luther said he would stay up and make sure everything was OK, and that Daddy and I should start for home. It would get us back just in time for Daddy to go down again. If we got back quickly, he might even make it to the barn and go down in soft straw in the inside coolness of the shaded place. We let the horses move at their homeward rate. We heard the Angelus bell and at this distance the bell strokes came layered instead of one by one, like sheets floating into folds, and for the first time we did not stop but overrode our own rule here where no one could see. Daddy doesn't talk much, but it was good to be with him. When he came to the place where you can see down to the house and barn and the first two fields of Croom Ranch, he stopped for a few seconds and said almost in a whisper, "Damn if she don't look fine."

And we did make the barn. I was sighing with relief, slipping down off Achsa, when I saw the wood cart moving up the road. Elise and Claire were coming in. For a split second I thought we had had another perfect day. The girls, nicely out of the way, had come back in time, Daddy had gotten free of the doctor, the secret of the longhorns was safe, and so were all the visitors, and here we were in time for supper and an innocent evening on the porch. We . . .

. . . Something was wrong with them. They couldn't seem to manage the cart. I couldn't see their faces yet at that distance, but they were walking like people who are holding bad pain very gently: a stiff walk but a blind one, and they had no hats on. Sunstroke, I thought. I began to make a move toward them. Daddy moved beside me. I wished he would go in and lie down before he fell. I told him I would take care of the horses. If they saw us from the house, Mama might come out here and bring the doctor. Daddy said, "Look at them girls."

I said, "They've got too much sun."

"Too much sun?" And he spat and said, "Them girls are tight as vat flies." He was standing in Nebby's shadow and then he went down in that boneless way he has, not a pitchover but a slide, gracefully almost. Louise calls it water-jointed.

I had a minute of panic. What if the doctor came now, or Dorothy, and there were the girls moving closer and obviously sick, although I couldn't believe what Daddy had said. I pulled at him. He was almost under Nebby's feet. I kept pulling him the few yards into the barn. I wanted to hide him, but I didn't know where. I couldn't get him to where the hay bales were, or to a clean stall of sweet straw. I left him behind the door, behind a hay bale, as near the north corner as I could get. Any nearer and he would wake up in a forest of tools and might bring one or two down on himself. Then I ran to Elise and Claire.

They *were* drunk. Their faces were hot and dry and for a moment again I thought it was sunstroke, but the smell of product was all over them. They had found the shebang. They could have been eating vat mash or drinking still-bottom. There's always product left here and there in the coils, making, or in test bottles left for empty. I just stood. I didn't know where to begin. People would be coming any minute to look for us now that the Angelus had rung. Supper. They could barely walk. They couldn't be seen at supper. Or smelled.

We had told Mr. Kelvin we would use only the pump for water, but there was a spigot in the barn, hidden now, by hay bales and boxes. I was a little clumsy, knocking over some tools, but I got busy and as I did I thought about Elise and Claire up at the shebang all day, drinking themselves blind or dead. I thought about them getting drunk and losing their way and going farther up the hill or to the river or over to the north edge of the land to fall down off the rocks that were there; any one of a dozen ways to be lost or hurt or to disappear or starve to death, while searchers combed the mountain in vain. My heart started to beat so fast I could hardly breathe. They were safe now, but what could have happened and what could happen again? As I came out with the water buckets, I saw Louise walking from the house. When she came up to us, she said, "Where have you been? We're all waiting supper."

I almost yelled at her: "The longhorns got out and these kids were at the shebang and are both drunk and Daddy's gone down and he's in the barn behind a hay bale and the doctor knows about his sleeps and wants to study him. How's that for a pleasant afternoon?"

She stood there for a moment and then said, "You don't deserve to lie there on the Cross like Jesus. You and Robert Luther have been trying to do this all alone. Don't expect 'Oh, poor girl' from me. Your way of keeping our secrets is splitting this family in half, into 'know' and 'don't know,' and if you think I'm happy being a don't know, you're nuts."

I wanted to kill her for a second but I saw her point, so I said, "It happened too quick to tell you, but now you *do* know, so what job do you want to take on?"

"I'll do the one walking the horses." And she climbed on Achsa and took Nebby by the bridle and went toward the house. I didn't know what she had in mind, but as she went I saw Robert Luther coming at the edge of the field.

We brought Balthazar in but did not unharness him, watching the two girls all the time. I told Robert Luther what must have happened. He thought if they worked as much as they could in the shade, they might exercise off some of what they had drunk, so we got them up from where they had been sitting and forced them, dizzy and sick, to help in walking the big horse, rubbing him down, and giving him water. Elise is a year younger than I am, big enough for real work. Drink had opened her up. She must have had a fine time up at the shebang. Most of that had worn off and she was hot and sick but she wasn't angry or fighting, only sick enough to do what we told her, "biddable" Daddy calls it. She said, "Follow me, horsey." Any horse following her would have needed six more legs. By the time Daddy came out of the barn, the girls were just beginning to sober up. They said they had headaches and wanted to heave, but they didn't. I wondered how much they had had to drink. We walked the horse until Louise came back with the doctor and the other horses and Mama's angry message to get in for dinner right away. I told the girls before the doctor got to us they had done all this to themselves, and if they complained or acted whiny, I would tell on them. "I don't like you very much," I said quickly, while Van Houghton and Louise were still out of earshot, "so don't tempt me." The girls were too sick to realize that they had us more than we had them. For a minute I was angry at Louise for bringing the doctor, but then I realized that she had kept him busy cooling off the horses until we had gotten things together. His attention was all on his job; he had barely noticed the girls. I thought all of us might just make it through dinner.

The girls held; I'll give them that. They fought nausea, sleep, dinner, and their own thick tongues. Mama and their folks were impressed with what they believed was dedication to the job, although Mama criticized Louise and Jane for letting them work so hard. No one mentioned or seemed to notice that they had only brought in one single load of wood all day. We could tell that the doctor was pleased. He thought their red faces, sleepiness, and lack of appetite were good indications of people getting in shape. Louise and I took them to bed after supper, and when we had done the dishes, Robert Luther said to us, "There's a pack-rat nest I found in the barn," and he took us out to see it, leaving the grown-ups on the porch, enjoying the sunset. Out of their sight, we told Louise and Jane everything that had happened.

Our secrets were lies, our lies excuses. We had made so many excuses protecting Daddy and explaining the drunken girls that when the real need came we were unprepared. The next morning I did the chores with Elise and Claire. I said it was to give them the experience of early morning in the barn. Actually it was to get them alone so that I could warn them both again that we were watching them and that they shouldn't go to the shebang anymore.

They looked awful, pale and sick, but they were their father's daughters. They didn't say anything. They clamped their teeth on the gritty glue in their mouths. I had heard about what comes from too much popscull. You could tell only by the careful way they put their feet down, walking, that they were suffering.

Maybe I went on too long, enjoying revenge, telling them all there was. We milked the cows, or I did, after they bent forward on their stools and swallowed sobs of pain. No punishment I ever had made me as sore and hurt as they were. No one would ask for pain like that, or do anything that would bring it on. They held their heads carefully as dancers or accident victims—carefully as I did when I was a kid and walked into a glass door at school. No one would choose that pain, I said to myself. I was wrong.

We moved around the heaved rumps of the milk cows to go and bucket-feed Achsa, Balthazar, and Nebby, and give them their hay. I was busy directing the girls because each horse ate different grain in different amounts and each had to be fed individually. That was why I missed the signs of Achsa's sickness at first.

I had heard her banging when we came in, a restlessness in the barn, but sometimes the horses did kick when the flies were deviling them. The noise had continued during milking but I was too absorbed in getting at the girls and doing the milking to notice. I passed Achsa with the bucket of feed for Nebby and I realized that all the sounds were coming from her. She was moving from foot to foot and something like a growl was coming from her throat. I watched her then, and as I did, getting more and more scared, she lay down and then as quickly got up again. I had seen horses, and cows, too, acting like that when they had the colic or had eaten loco weed. Where could she have gotten that? Then I remembered that Robert Luther and Dorothy had gone up to the fence line yesterday, checking fence. I tried to see in my mind exactly what was up there, something that Robert Luther was too love-happy to look for. It was a cutover place. Baneberry? Hemlock? Loco? I couldn't see, in my memory, anything more than the fence, the pasture, the woods on the other side. I tried to look close. It all blurred in my mind. I told Elise to get back to the house quick and get Daddy. She and Claire began to move together and I said, "Wait—not her; just you, and make it fast." I knew they would have to be separated from now on. They wouldn't want to make the trip to the shebang alone. I was pleasantly surprised that I had thought of that. Elise barely moved. "If you don't get going," I said, "I'm going to pull you out under the Angelus bell and ring it fifteen times right over your head."

People with hangovers hate noise. I learned that from TV. She went, then.

Daddy came, and the doctor, and Dorothy. Achsa was groaning deep in her throat. "It's poison, all right," Daddy said. "Look at how bloated she is, too."

"She was up at the fence line of the south pasture yesterday," I said. "Robert Luther and Dorothy were checking fence."

"Well, yes," Daddy said, sounding doubtful. "Two-groove vetch, maybe, loco. Hemlock grows in the draws, closer to water, but a horse won't eat any of them things unless there's just about nothing else for him to eat, and Robert Luther would have been there all along and would have seen her eating that, wouldn't he?" I didn't say anything. If Robert Luther was with Dorothy Van Houghton, he would be too google-eyed with puppy love to notice anything. That horse could have been eating haywire or Mama's chocolate eclairs and he wouldn't have known the difference. Daddy walked around to Achsa's head and put his face close to her mouth. He said, "Sometimes you can—" and he leaned in even closer and said, "Well, that's it."

"What?"

"It ain't loco weed at all."

The doctor looked amused, that snooty look I hated. I wanted to kick him in the pants. He said, "How can you tell what it is?"

"Smell her breath; it's gassy. This horse has got to some gasoline or white gas, or . . . or kerosene."

"What will you do?" The doctor was interested now.

"Nothin' you *can* do but keep her movin', keep her up. I seen this before, years ago at a county fair—contaminated feed. They had to walk the horses back and forth all day. They give 'em pain pills, too."

"Pain pills?" Dorothy had not spoken before. She had been standing in back of us all and a little away.

"Sure," Daddy said, "this horse has the same kind of

151

bellyache you'd get if *you* had a shot glass of kerosene with your dinner."

"I think I can help, then," she said, and she turned away and walked out of the barn.

We tried to get Achsa to drink, and then Daddy haltered her and we had to pull her outside because she wanted to stay in her stall. Twice she lay down and we had all we could do to get her up again, pulling and lifting and yelling at her. She kept groaning; she all but cried. When we came outside Dorothy was there with one of those plastic bottles of medicine they give you with prescriptions. She said, "This isn't from the 1880s, but maybe we could stretch a point this once." Daddy asked her what it was. "Valium," she said.

I saw the doctor look at her. He began to say something and then changed his mind and turned to Daddy and said, "It should take care of part of the pain at least."

"How much should she have?"

The doctor took the bottle and asked questions about Achsa's weight and age. It was then I looked around and saw that the girls had gone.

I felt like the worst fool there is. I had sworn the four of us to watch them and keep them here, away from the shebang. The day hadn't half begun and they were gone and I had been fooled again, left angry and ashamed with nothing to do but be quiet and wait until I was alone with Robert Luther so we could make a plan.

The grown-ups decided how much Valium would help a horse, gave it, and then Daddy tried to find out how Achsa had gotten the contaminated feed in the first place. As soon as I thought back, I remembered Daddy's sleep yesterday after Angelus. I remembered how confused and clumsy I had been, how I had pulled him into the barn and over to the space behind the hay bale. I remembered getting water to sober up the girls. It was while I was getting to the water that I upset the lantern

152

on a bale. Later I saw it was there and picked it up and hung it back on its nail out of the way, not thinking how much of its kerosene might have soaked into the hay. Daddy must have used the bale to get it out of the way. It was I who had hurt Achsa, not the visitors, which was what I knew Daddy had been thinking. I wanted him to think so. They had put us through so much. Finally, I sighed and told him that I had upset the lantern while I was working and hadn't noticed it until later and that I hadn't realized the kerosene would leak out and sink into Achsa's hay.

Daddy didn't yell at me in front of the visitors. He knew I felt bad about Achsa and ashamed that the simple life of the 1880s had fooled me with its new dangers. When I lived in the twentieth century I had to learn not to leave electric irons on. Now in the nineteenth, there were other things; lots of things. I thought of the girls up at the shebang. I knew I should tell someone; I couldn't. Daddy told me to walk Achsa back and forth and not to let her lie down, and to call him if she lay down and wouldn't get up again. He was proud of me for being honest about the kerosene. I felt worse for not telling about the girls. I tried to signal Daddy with my eyes when the doctor and Dorothy were looking the other way. I tried to get Robert Luther's attention and signal to him, but they all trooped off and I was left alone to tell my troubles to the poor horse, who, thanks to me, had troubles of her own.

It got a lot hotter in front of the barn, walking back and forth, up and down. As the morning passed and Achsa and I kept moving, I had plenty of time to imagine what was happening to Elise and Claire up at the shebang. For the last three days they had been drinking all afternoon. Now they would have all day to drink. Could you die from it? I thought I had heard of that happening.

I thought maybe I could get away at lunch. When

153

noon came, I walked Achsa to the house. Dorothy was there with Mama and Jane, so I couldn't say anything. She said she planned to go up to the high pasture with Robert Luther to set up salt licks. Louise was working with Daddy and the doctor in the south field. If the doctor started asking Daddy about his sleeps, she would begin with her favorite subjects—word history or what a sonnet is. She can do forty-five minutes without stopping. They had taken a picnic basket to eat in the field. Daddy's sleep wasn't due until three o'clock. At two-thirty Louise was supposed to remind him to come back and check on Achsa. That left Jane and Mama. Now, they were all canning rhubarb and mint jelly, telling stories, and they had created a kitchen mess that would take hours to work their way through. Two pie crusts lay waiting to be filled. The canner water was heating, the jar-washing water was heating, the kitchen was asteam. Mama couldn't go after those dumb girls; neither could Jane. I went out and got Achsa again and saw the Van Houghton girls in my mind, slipping into their darkness. I had warned them; so had Robert Luther. Elise wasn't a baby. Now I would have to wait until after lunch.

At two-thirty I went to the house again and Mama waved a hand at me and said, "Fix yourself a sandwich, honey. Dorothy has eaten already and gone up to the pasture with Robert Luther. Pity them both in all this heat."

"It's warmer in here, but I'm glad to be alone with you. I'm sick of that family tangled up in our secrets. The doctor knows about Daddy and Dorothy knows about the longhorns." I didn't mention the girls, but in keeping one secret, I had blundered into another.

Mama gave a yell. "Good Lord, darlin', what if Dorothy tells someone. We'll all go to jail and they'll throw us off the SCELP!" I wanted to tell her we were nearer ruin than that. I ate my sandwich—cold venison—and went back out.

154

The poor sick horse picked up a little in the afternoon. I had more of Dorothy's Valium pills, and for a minute I thought of taking a couple myself. Achsa always liked me to sing to her, so I sang while I walked her, whatever came to mind, even songs Mama sang to us, like "Bye, Bye Blackbird," which *her* mother had taught her. I was tired and sad and my voice sounded it, but it did keep the pictures out of my mind: Elise and Claire, where were they? Elise and Claire, how were they—lost or wandering into some impossible trouble or other?

I heard them first—a sound on the road, carried by the rising heat. Although the home field had been cut and the second field was being seeded, I couldn't see the road from where I was standing, but there was something—I thought at first that hope was doing it, the way a phone call you are waiting for sounds the bell that isn't ringing. Then, in a little dip the road takes, I saw, or thought I saw, a flash of color. I walked Achsa quickly toward the place the road came out. She was surprised by the speed, and a little insulted. She shook and gave a whinny.

They looked as though they had run all the way, fallen, gotten up and run again. Their clothes were filthy, their faces streaked, their hair was matted and pulled in wisps from their ponytails. I left Achsa and ran toward them. "What happened?" For a moment they stopped and stared at me, swaying, unable to answer, and then they ran again, closing the space. "What is it?"

As we came closer together, I could see panic on their faces. "What is it?" I said again. This time I yelled, and Claire, younger and too scared to hold it in, rasped out, "The Death Eater—the giant in the story"—trying for breath—"he was there—we saw him there—the giant who has no face!"

One Eye. When I understood, I almost laughed. The two of them up there had probably scared him as much as he had scared them. Then . . . I thought of the ugly little jokes he liked to make when we were alone; the way he looked at me, the suggestions over other people's heads about my body . . . "Miss Kate, anyone would like you as a little cupcake for dessert." Cupcake—could he have said that to them—could he have done something? Hurt them? I looked at their clothes. They were wearing jeans and blouses. The clothes had been snagged on things, but were not ripped. I knew that if they had been very frightened of him, they would have done whatever he demanded. "What happened?" I had trouble breathing and my voice was odd. I had tried to make it very hard and grown-up so they would stop seeing me as just another kid. They stood trembling with the memory, still struggling for breath. I said, "Well?" and that sounded better.

Elise began, a few words at a time. "He had no face . . . he kept hiding behind trees . . . leaping out . . . chasing us. He said he . . . would boil us in the big pot and eat us. He said . . . some parts he would eat . . . other parts he would save to play with . . . and then he laughed . . ."

"And?"

"And . . . then we got away."

For a minute I stood looking at them and didn't talk. I knew I could tell them anything I wanted, including that they had dreamed it all, that popscull does that to people. I didn't like them and now I was angry at what they had put us through. Last night Louise had complained that guarding them and protecting their secret had split the family in a way that none of our other secrets did. One Eye had scared and menaced them for his own fun, maybe, but he had done us a favor. He was better than snakes, lightning, or bears. So I said, "That man is a little crazy. He lives up in those woods. He hates people. He's called One Eye." Then I shut my mouth, and didn't say any more for a minute or two, letting it soak in. Then

I asked them if they were drunk. They hung their heads. "You're going to have to walk it off—this horse is as drunk as you are. You are going to have to walk each other sober until Angelus or until Daddy says to stop. Mama will be looking at you from the house. If you fake out or stop walking she'll tell your folks what sneaks you are."

I knew at that minute that I couldn't stay around them anymore. If I did, I would only be angrier. I decided it would be better if I went up and did some sensible work with Dorothy and Robert Luther, using the walk to the high pasture, which was a couple of miles, to calm me down. It was hard work, that walk, up to the top of the hill, but at the end a person could look out at other mountains riding away and away into the blue distance and feel the order of them, the rhythm, and be quieted. It always calmed me down. That hilltop is my favorite place.

They would be finished setting the salt licks by now and would probably be making sure of the place where the longhorns had broken through the fence. Cattle sometimes try again where they have once gone through. And I had to admit there was something less decent in my wanting to be with them. I had a small, slow-burning little envy at the way Robert Luther looked-did-not-look at Dorothy Van Houghton, and at the way he followed her secretly with his eyes. I walked uphill, using the work to get rid of my anger at those stupid girls, keeping in the shade as much as I could.

I was glad I had decided to do it; it was a long, hot walk and the heat watered over the trees to the east, but it was good to get away from everyone for a while. As I walked, I tried to get rid of the Van Houghton girls and the doctor trying to get Daddy's secrets and the nervousness that came from our having to meet new people every week and the sudden possibilities good and bad we had never thought about when we had decided to go on the program. I thought our family needed to be alone for a while to think about it all, to get our minds clear enough to know what we all thought now. There wasn't time. The visitors were coming one after another and no letup in sight and no time to protect ourselves from the bad ones or learn how from the good ones. All I had now were feelings, mostly angry, at what had happened to us. I tried to remember back to the winter when we had had so much fun with the Lundgrens and the Teeters and the Paynes, and how much we had liked them and how much they had appreciated what we were doing. They had said anyone would. They had also encouraged us about the program saving the ranch. A special niche for a special place, Mr. Teeter had said. I had thought to myself then that if things worked out, we could make enough so we wouldn't have to depend on popscull and deer jacking, which made us dependent on One Eye. None of us liked One Eye except Daddy. I thought of him and the girls again, and wondered if I should tell Robert Luther as soon as I could. It made me boil to think about it. Through all the visitors, Daddy and Robert Luther had to creep away to check things at the shebang. Between visitors, shebang work was mostly what they did. Then there was this business with the girls. I knew One Eye was angry at us about the SCELP program, and his nervousness had gotten worse since that club of his got started. Another run was due again soon, this time between visitors, so we didn't have to pull the usual playact about returning defective product. To add to the mess, Daddy was so busy and needed One Eye's money so much, and Robert Luther was so taken up with the daily work of the visitors, that I didn't know if they would take me seriously, would really listen to me. The shebang would have to be moved, the visitors kept safe. I was thinking about all of this as I was walking up and turning the mountain away from the ranch and up to where the highest pasture was and the woods took over.

I heard their voices, a quick laugh from the woods, and a word or two of Robert Luther's. I heard a horse snort and stamp. I walked more quickly toward the place the sounds had come from. They must have gone into the woods to rest and be sitting against trees out of the eye of the sun. I came to the horses tied up to tree branches in the shade just at the pasture's edge. I walked on and didn't hear them and was about to call out when I came a step or two and saw them. They were on the ground together, twenty or thirty feet from where I was. They were not completely undressed, but mostly, and they were wound up on one another, arms and legs twined and very white against the clothes they had put down to keep them from the pine-duff under the trees.

It was a dappled place, sun and shadow, but dry and still hot. They were stroking one another and talking, doing and not doing, and they were completely *with* one another. I felt as though they wouldn't be able to hear me if I fired a cannon to call them. They were domed over in a little world all their own. It was a world no bigger than themselves. I stood, staring, until very suddenly I saw myself seeing them. Spying. It made me feel guilty of something and angry at myself for feeling that way and angry at them for doing what they were doing and angry at her—at that damn Dorothy.

I backed away, trying to keep my feet soft in the dry pine needles, and when I was safe behind the horses I turned and ran. All of a sudden, for no reason, I started to cry. I cried as I ran, trying to cry less so I could see to run. Because of the way the land sloped, there was a natural pull toward the lower pasture, toward home.

It was the last place I wanted to be. I caught myself, headlong down the hill, and stopped in the middle of the third field that Daddy and the doctor had just seeded. At the bottom of it I could see them, walking the seeder in the slow, even way that the doctor had spent so much time trying to "improve" when Daddy first showed him. I hated the doctor, just then. He had brought that woman and those damn children up here to separate us from one another, to make us feel wrong about everything. I hated myself, too. Robert Luther had grown away because of them, slipped away into the grown-up world without any warning at all. And she was old—old enough to be his mother. When had he started to be a man? It must have been happening all along. I remembered his body as it was there in the dappled light, a man's body, fully grown, with hair and the details boys' bodies don't have. Too late to catch him. When had his feet grown so big? Why hadn't I noticed his tread changing from boy's to man's, his hands growing with the work he did? Now it was too late to say good-bye; he had gone beyond me and away. I sat down for a minute on the soft ground. I was frightened and sad and angry. Each feeling seemed to come one after the other without reason, without words. What would happen when I saw Robert Luther and Dorothy Van Houghton again, how could I greet them and talk to them in the ordinary way? It wasn't only that I had seen them together, lying in the pine duff, his hands on her, and it wasn't only that this was one more secret. It was about his changed nature. Under the shirt, which would be buttoned when I saw him next, and the pants, neatly held with galluses, would be not a boy's body but a man's. I wouldn't know how to talk to that man. I would stutter or be dumb. And she would know I knew. It would show on me; it had to. I got up, afraid to cry again, and went toward the house, avoiding the girls who were still walking Achsa up and down. There was no place to go but home, no one to see but Mama. I was tired of being stuck in this asylum, where anything might drive the inmates to more craziness. The girls might still go back

160

to the shebang. The doctor might still force Daddy to tell about his sleeps. Last night he had tried to get Mama to tell him about the Fleuris. Dorothy might let loose about the longhorns or what she had done with Robert Luther. *He* was drunk with love and the crazy girls were drunk with popscull and I wanted everything to be back the way it was when the only secrets we had were from the government.

Inside the house I heard men's voices. I stopped. I didn't want to face any more surprises. If Louise hadn't headed Daddy off at two-thirty, the way she was supposed to, and he had fallen over asleep, he and the doctor would probably be in there now. We were not supposed to have watches on SCELP, but all of us did. We carried them in our pockets and looked at them for Daddy's sleeps or coming home for Angelus. I looked at my watch now. It was after four. I came closer and heard that the voices were not Daddy's or the doctor's. SCELP people maybe, or people from the Ags or the Forest Service or the Farm Bureau or someplace else. Maybe some agency was checking Daddy's deer. There was a doe still hanging in the secret cellar under the barn. Then I heard a burst of music and I realized what it was and laughed and came into the kitchen and Mama, guilty and quick, dropped her little battery-operated radio into the cooling stove as though it was paper on fire. She hadn't had time to turn it off and we could hear the music coming through the ash, and echoing in the iron chamber of the range.

"Mama," I said, "you better get those poor men out of that ash box before they start coughing, and we have the Health Department or the OSHA out here."

"Good Lord, Kate, it's only you!" And Mama looked down into the range hole and then she had to go feeling around in the still-warm ashes for the radio. "Bein' here all alone I thought I'd get a little nice music. Jane went to warn your daddy and she's probably coolin' off now in

161

the barn or she's under the house makin' straw people. Louise went up to the pasture just now to get Robert Luther."

My mouth went dry. "Why?"

"Silliness, really. Jane fell asleep after lunch and had a dream about the longhorns and their calves and she started worryin' because when the longhorns got out yesterday, Robert Luther didn't see all their calves with them."

She went on talking about Jane and the longhorn calves. I sat down on the kitchen stool. It was too late to head off Louise. If she found Robert Luther and Dorothy making love up there, it would just have to happen. I was too tired to care anymore. I started to cry . . .

"Darlin' girl!" Mama ran arms out to me. "What's wrong?"

I wanted to tell her but I only said, "Oh, I'm just tired and sick of the Van Houghtons, all of them, and I wish they'd all go home and I wish I had a vacation from 1880s life and 1980s visitors."

What Mama calls her mother strings tightened up in her and she sat down on the other kitchen stool and started to cry, too. We sat there together in the hot kitchen and bawled for a good fifteen minutes, and then she got up and went out on the back step and got the jar of sun tea she had there and poured us each a glass. We sat and drank it and got quiet, and then she looked around and groaned. "This kitchen is a mess, Kate."

"I know. Do you want me to help clean it up?"

"Why don't you send those useless girls in?"

"I will. It was nice to sit here with you for a while, though." She asked me if I wanted some school friends up. "Most of them have gone to camp or foreign countries. Cimi is actually on a SCELP program with an Indian tribe somewhere in the East."

Then Mama began to spin the dream that I had secretly been dreaming. It made me know that the phys. ed. teacher was wrong and that she really does have mother strings. "Kate, some fall day, when everything is glowing and the high aspen are copper-gold and the grove aspen are sun-gold and you can taste the air, we're goin' to get a family who are happy people. They'll have lovely sweet girls and bright handsome boys. They'll have a really good time here, and Robert Luther and you will be good friends with them and you'll write to each other after, and then next year they'll be back, or in different seasons, and maybe in a few years we'll have some weddings up here, and since this is me dreaming, I'm gonna say they'll come on the SCELP with us and this will be a real famous program—sheep and cattle and wool spinning and tanning and I'll get to have yours and Robert Luther's babies to watch comin' up."

It sounded dumb and romantic when Mama said it. She knew how to dream with us, and even when the dreams were silly, we knew she could see under the silliness to where the hope was not silly at all. "Mama, that will never happen in this world."

Then Mama laughed. "Maybe if we both wish and pray real hard, it will."

"If I send Claire and Elise in to you, will you make them do something in this kitchen?"

"I'll send 'em upstairs to sleep."

I went out to where the girls were supposed to be walking Achsa. They were fast asleep on their feet. Elise was sleeping standing up, with Achsa's reins in her hand, leaning against Achsa and Achsa was leaning against the barn wall. Claire was hung over the feed box, boneless as a cat. The girls still stank of booze and sweat and sick horse. I woke them up and told them to go in the house and let Mama wash them. I watched them go. Achsa was sleeping, too. I sat against the barn wall and soon I was almost sleeping myself.

I was saved from seeing Robert Luther as a stranger. The next time I saw him he was shaking me awake, as though he had not gone past me at all and out of sight into that other world. Before I knew any more than that, I was telling him about what One Eye had done to the girls.

"He didn't hurt them, did he?"

"I don't think he even touched them, but I can't be sure."

"We'll have to move the shebang."

I almost cried with gratitude. He had heard me, really heard. It was like things were before.

"It's time anyway; the tree cover around there is all gone and everything is bare. It's a wonder people haven't found it before now," he said. "I'll tell Dad."

"I don't like having One Eye up there." I made my voice serious and slow.

Robert Luther shrugged. "He goes up with charcoal and supplies now and then. Sometimes he cuts wood and stacks it so we can speed up our runs. It's only once a month or so."

"How do we know how often he comes? I'm scared of being alone with him up there—if I go out after mushrooms or just for a walk."

"Has he done anything?"

"It's the way he talks to me."

"I'll tell him I know about that and if I hear anything more . . ."

The girls did not go to the shebang again. They stayed their last two days around the house, helping Mama, dumb and grim. Now and then I felt sorry for them. With the worry of them gone, I had more time to watch Robert Luther hurting, aching, and yearning for Dorothy Van Houghton. She had her own quick looks at him when she thought no one was watching. They had spun something between them, invisible strands that pulled their eyes and hands toward one another without their knowing they were doing it—there was a kind of attraction in the molecules of their air—a force they couldn't deny, and I saw him measure out the hours and the minutes of her time at the Croom and I saw his eyes go blank with loss. I was glad when they all left. I thought the doctor was a stuffy and selfish man, and that she was a loose and selfish woman. And she was too old, with her dyed hair and her soft body jiggling and wiggling after Robert Luther. I thought their kids were sour and mean when they weren't almost dead drunk. I knew I would feel more for them later, as the hurt they had given us faded away. I knew, too, that I thought hard things about them because if I didn't, the sorrow of them would make me cry, the way the loss of Robert Luther had.

16

Robert Luther

I never had a woman before; I fooled around with girls; I had crushes and hungers; I did backseat stuff. I did half of it because it was someway expected. I was stuck on Mary Blascovic, but she plays "giving herself" bit by bit, and it's not loving; it's not even liking. Dorothy was married and that makes what we did a sin no matter what she said. But, I couldn't wait for more. For a minute when I found the longhorn breakout and after when Kate told me that Dorothy's dumb little girls were both drunk, I thought there was some kind of message in it—not like getting struck by lightning, but like a sign that when people break rules, something happens to everyone; one of the strings that holds the world in place gets untied. I know we're not supposed to think like that; it's not scientific. In school they tell you to be scientific in your thinking, but early in the morning when the sky is hot and hollow with drought even at dawn and the hoppers are popping a month too soon in the shackleweed—a sound I hate because it is so brainless and scary—I don't only think about the science of things. I think about the different times we made love and what I learned. I already knew about the scientific part of making love, but Dorothy gave a meaning to all of it. Sometimes the memory is sad and sometimes funny, but mostly it just aches. I wonder if she and I didn't set up what happened to Croom Ranch in the weeks after they left.

Dad and I spent the day after their leaving locating a new site for the shebang and the next day, almost all day, we moved it; the boilers and the coils and the collector and the knockdown walls of the structure. We took it farther up the Croom and over south across the road where it was harder to get to and harder to find. Even a bad path, well-worn, gets easy, and the wood around the new spot would keep us in fire for quite a time. We came back exhausted and we thought, like every hopeful criminal in the country, I guess, that we had solved the thing.

I was glad for the work. I wanted to work until I couldn't see. Dorothy had trained my body to want her and life had trained me to be guilty for having her, a wife and a mother. I went over all the things she had said and now they sounded different to me than they had when she said them. They sounded like excuses, not reasons. And my body hungered for her and I was ready ten times a day just thinking about her, so I wanted to kill my ache with work. Everyone else, even Jane, was glad when they were all gone. They laughed at Dr. Van Houghton, running after Dad, and those two silly girls. It was hard to believe they had really been that drunk. Of course, no one mentioned product, just sun. Mama believed it: "Those girls were nigh-on sick with all that sun," she said, "and rest is the thing for that." I knew they had been a handful, but not for me. I had escaped the trouble they gave.

One Eye came two days later, pounding the Angelus

bell as though there were a forest fire. "Where the holy hell did you put the goddamn shebang at!" We told about moving it because the wood nearby had been used up and SCELP visitors were finding the place and getting more of an 1880s experience up at it than the government would have wanted. "Them girls!" he shouted into my face, "them damn drunken girls!" It took me by surprise. I had expected to worm that out of him and his coming out with it, his anger, put me off. It seemed to say that he hadn't been guilty of hurting the girls; a guilty person tries to keep what he has done a secret. He couldn't have known that they were going to tell us. . . . He was muttering about them.

"What did you do it for?" I asked him. "Why did you scare them like that?"

"Why not? I don't like kids for the first thing; I don't like kids in my business for the second; I don't like the damn SCALP for the third; and . . ."

He was doing his best act: Don't Tread On Me, with the burned side of his face turned our way, swearing and menacing, standing close to us with his fists doubled up, talking into our faces. I would have been nervous but I'd seen it too many times before, even though this was a number-one attempt. Then up drove Kelvin.

I could see Kelvin's annoyance even from the car, and One Eye's presence didn't help. Of course Kelvin is not allowed to choose who comes here except for people on the program, but I knew he was curious about One Eye and put off by him. Most people are. Dad and I told Kelvin One Eye was a neighbor who made up a cattle dip we used and had a lot of old-time knowledge, and that he had saved many of the out-of-stock parts of the machinery we used. They dipped their heads at one another and didn't say any more. I expected One Eye to leave, but he stood looking at me while Dad, who had been standing beside me, tried to figure out what was

168

going on. Dad knew about the girls being up at the she-bang but not about One Eye menacing them, playing Giant Without a Face. The whole conversation slid into a nervous kind of code.

ONE EYE: "Well, where is the damn wood lot now?"

DAD: "Uphill, a quarter-mile south of the old one. There are lots of trees for the takin'. We'll show you."

ME: "Christmas trees and deadwood for fires."

ONE EYE: "It'll kill my truck gettin' there. There ain't no road."

DAD: "There's a good way in to mebbe six hundred feet. Later we'll clear some of the rough parts so your wood truck can come in closer."

ONE EYE: "I can't get Christmas trees out without spoilin' 'em."

ME: "By Christmas we'll have made it easier."

ONE EYE: "And I don't want no one comin' up and gettin' in the way of my wood cuttin'. It ain't safe, trees fallin' and that."

DAD: "That ain't gonna happen, which is a reason we are movin' it out of the way."

ONE EYE: "I'll yell at 'em if they come."

ME: "You can tell us when you go up there. Stop in for a bit."

DAD: "The new lot's on the other side of the road from where it was. There's gates to open. Let's go next time and I'll show you."

One Eye was in a worse than sour mood about it all. You could see that. Still, he had no choice but to get in his truck, slam the gears until they screeched, and blaze away, bumping and bucking before his dust-up down the road. Mama and the girls saw him go. They came out and we all gathered in front of Kelvin.

His gripe was the same. We had been praying. He told us that five separate people had mentioned it on their Post Placement sheets. Even though most of them had praised it, it would have to stop, he said. We told him we had stopped the Sunday Bible reading when he first took against the idea, but that everyone seemed to like the Angelus and no one *had* to say any prayer or even amen. The visitors didn't even have to stop work—they only did because we did—and they didn't have to bow their heads—they only did it because we did. We had gotten the grace back to a simple "Thank You for the food before us and the day behind us" at dinner.

Kelvin heard the grace and nearly came apart. "Don't you see that the 'You' in that prayer refers to God? Besides, the whole thing shows gratitude. Gratitude is the opening wedge. You'll be ending up with the doxology!"

Dad said, "I didn't say it was God. Could be Father Time, Santy Claus . . . Rudolph."

"Rudolph?"

"That reindeer; the one the City of Denver can put up on the courthouse lawn every Christmas instead of Baby Jesus."

"You cannot be seen praying; I told you that before. You can *say* you pray. At supper, if you don't say *anything* you can sit still for a minute, and I have gotten the administration to allow you to stop at that bell you use, and to say 'We stop.' Just that for the bell and for the table grace: 'We stop.' That's all."

I could tell Dad was getting worked up. He said to Kelvin, "You know this-all is for Mary Beth. That woman didn't get a single awning or flowerpot or Japanese lantern or lawn party or grape arbor out of all this. She's give up her stove and freezer-refrigerator, washer and TV, and not to mention her woman's beauty mess, curlers and that. All that she's give up without a whimper, well without hardly, and she's took all kinds of garbage off of kids and people angry because they was promised the miracle of birth and ended up gettin' the miracle of death instead, and took it out on her." I was surprised and proud. Dad talked more in the 1880s than he had in the 1980s. "Let me tell you about Mary Beth," Dad said. "Most people got nothin' in their mind but gettin' more of whatever it is they want. I seen that here in Bascom High in 1962. Deep down in Mary Beth is a idea of the way people and things ought to be. It don't have to do with money or class. She runs true. Now, if she wants us to stick feathers on and set in the field and cluck like a chicken, it's okay with me."

"This is a constitutional, a federal government, issue."

"This is a issue of what Mary Beth wants to do at her own goddamn table. Pardon my French."

They stood and eyed one another and then Kelvin changed his attack. He started in on what he called our "encumbrance." That's the money we ask for. The socks, hats, food, the emergency phone Doctor Van Houghton wanted hidden away in secret somewhere in case there was a fire or an emergency up here. It went on and on, our list. He told us all about the other placements that were doing so much better at keeping their encumbrances down. Mama was out by that time with some cookies and grape juice and as she came by she whispered to me, "Sounds like what mamas do to kids when they want 'em to act nice: See how good your brother is actin'." I laughed. He was telling us about the Chicano placements in the Denver ghetto and the American Indian placements on the eastern plains. We stood there and took it all and it seemed to make him angry.

He said, "Don't think I haven't fought for you. Don't think I haven't gone down there and defended these stupid requisitions of yours. You've got to stop making more and you've got to stop making trouble with hats, a hundred hats, and prayers and hunting and trapping. You can be authentic but not authentically illegal. We have domesticated the past; that's what SCELP is. Why don't you realize that *authentic* doesn't mean *real*?"

171

Mama said, "Don't it? I thought it did."

Kelvin had the bit in his teeth. "No, it doesn't, and no one knows it better than you. The real past lost its young in childbirth and had diseases we have banished. It drank diseased milk and went scorbutic every winter in all classes of society; it lost its teeth early and had rickets. It hated blacks and said epilepsy was caused by masturbation. The real past was ridden with superstititon and ignorance. That past is well dead, well gone."

We just stood there and listened to him go. He told us his dream was that people would learn to remake their pasts, to correct them, and, having learned better, to hold the *corrected* past as a kind of escape route when the present got too bad. It must not be polluted as we had polluted the present, he said; it must not be spoiled by what spoils the present: greed, fear, and violence. He stopped then, seeing we didn't understand most of what he was saying. Then Jane said, "Does that mean we're supposed to stop doing product, too?"

There was that long wait that happens when everyone is hanging in his own part of a shock and is voiceless, and Jane said again, "Mr. Kelvin, does that mean we should stop running product? I hope so, because it's making everyone be too busy and too tired."

We all knew someone should do something. I tried to think quickly. Running product. She hadn't said the worst word yet. I went over and picked her up and put her on my shoulders and said, "We have to have products, Janie, all the products we make up here on Croom by ourselves and with the visitors." She began to explain so I had to carry her away into the house as though we were funning. Once we were alone, I tried to tell her very gently how to keep her trap shut. I told her to make another picture for Mr. Kelvin, but she said, "I'm sad about him. He has changed a lot and he gets angry at you and Daddy." I told her that everyone was trying to work things out right and do the best for all of us. I reminded her that product was a secret. She said, "I forgot, Robert Luther. It's like jacking deer and the long-horns and the funny way people used to treat us and the other funny way they treat us now?" I said yes, but it surprised me and made me sad. I had forgotten that Janie had seen and felt those things. I wondered what she meant by the "funny way they treat us now." There wasn't time to go into it. I knew how she felt, wanting to defend us, even though she hadn't done any of the things Kelvin was complaining of. It was hard to tell him, for example, that my hats were important to me, that when I found the right one, the one that demonstrated *me*, I would settle and be happy and would need no more. It wasn't the cost of them he hated, it was the want itself, the encumbrance, the justifying to his bosses. But it was so little; why couldn't they see? Kelvin was still outside and I knew One Eye would be back soon to yell on about us making more popscull. We were to have new visitors, too. I wanted some idea of them. And there was still the matter of having to ask for more horses—three more, at least, and right after Kelvin had told us we couldn't ask for *anything*. It all pointed to more popscull and more deer jacking. Anyone could see that. I left Jane in the parlor. I tried to remember to ask her about what she had said, but in the end I forgot.

Because hanging over me like the mist that covers the Croom in March and the fogs and clouds of October was the memory of Dorothy and the sting of my new need, keen as a wet rope end when it snaps back across your hand or stings your cheek, and patient as toothache. Body and soul I hungered for that woman, for her pulses under my fingers and her body wide open to receive me, to take me in and hold me inside her. I wanted to re-member it all, not to let any of it go. After we had been together twice, she asked me what the most demanding job on the Croom was. I said pitching hay. She said, "Not hardest, most demanding." I said herding longhorns because you have to be calm and concerned with all their moves, trying to outguess them. She said, "You're not reasoning then, you're *being*." I said I guess so. She said, "Then make love the way you herd longhorns," and we laughed because we both knew herding was also hot, dusty, sweaty, and exasperating. I wanted to relive all we had said and done, and think about it, to remember it in detail, but it was summer, and the work of summer was there to be done.

Kelvin was back a few days later and the next week he came again to give us the papers on the new visitors we would be getting a few days after that. When the going gets tough, he gets psychological. This time he talked about dependency. He said that dependency was our enemy and that it led to passive-aggressive behavior that was counterproductive. Dad asked him to put that into English. I suspected Kelvin had been to some kind of training program between visits—something to do with "motivating" us to do things right. He said, "It's about you having to ask and my having to turn you down time after time. It builds up resentment. Every denial I have to make of what you think is a reasonable encumbrance request increases your dependency ambivalence and our resentment. You become bitter over your loss of autonomy." There was a truth to what he said even though I didn't understand it all.

Then Mama said, "Mr. Kelvin, why don't we make peace just like they did in the old-timey days? Why don't we have a party?"

Kelvin almost went pale. I could see him say to the program director in his mind, "You don't know the kind of people I deal with . . ."

Mama went on. "I don't mean a big expense or nothin' like that. I thought we could invite you and all the people

174

we're friends with in Bascom up here on July Fourth. We could tell them there'd be a hayride and a place to picnic. We have a flag somewhere and we could make a flag the way it was in 1880 and just not spend any money at all, but have an 1880 Fourth of July." She got the last word up like a question.

Mr. Kelvin wrinkled up his face. "It never starts out costing money with you people," he said, "but it always ends up . . ." and he trailed off with his voice and a gesture that made me choose between "passive-aggressive" and plain fighting mad. We all stood around for a minute trying to recover ourselves. With all the trouble and the covering up and lying and double-tracking we'd been doing, we had forgotten the simple purpose of SCELP, the simple gifts. Mama was the only one who had really been living the program, and we knew that back there with her heavy washpots and soap boxes and ash leachers she had been thinking this out in a way Mama seldom does. Mr. Kelvin opened his mouth to say no, but Dad moved right in.

"I told you this woman had no rose arbor," he said, "no patio nor Japanese lanterns." He stared Mr. Kelvin down.

"It can't be permitted to cost any money," Mr. Kelvin said. "Not a cent. Agreed?"

"Agreed."

"And no praying and no single mention of You-Know-Who. Not one."

"Agreed."

"And no hunting for barbecue. None. Not a quail or wild turkey or even so much as a squirrel. Agreed?"

"Agreed."

"And no controlled substances, no hint of anything illegal. Agreed?"

"Agreed."

"Because there have been rumors," Mr. Kelvin said,

175

"I might as well tell you. And no games of chance or penny matching. None of that."

"Good God, man!" And Dad shook his head. "What do you think we are, road artists? You got a deep mind, Ralph. It's that government work that's made you that way. There's another thing we ain't gonna do and that's set folks out under the trees over on the east there and give 'em all Mickey Finns in their iced tea and rob their pockets while they are sleepin'."

Mr. Kelvin stared at Dad after that and then without saying a word, just nodded. Mama would have her Fourth of July.

It made us feel a little better about the things that had happened to us on SCELP. July Fourth was a celebration of independence. Even though we had lost most of ours, we still had a feeling about the way things should be. Mama started making a big plan for the 1880s American flag. Dad and I planned to move hay bales around the outside of the home field for people to sit on. We planned for two or three water barrels and we went and pulled out the harnesses for the hay wagon, early for the season. We took the wagon and pulled it in under the haymow, where we could fill it easily when the day came. All the time I worked I thought about Dorothy Van Houghton, wondering when I would stop suffering the want of her. Does need ever get tired and lie down and sleep?

The Leiths came that week for three days. They were so quiet and timid that they scurried around whispering, as though they were afraid of being caught in what they thought was a foreign time among foreign people. They were afraid of our sickles and harrows, our dressing knives and hay hooks. Louise said they had all been reincarnated from field mice who still remembered their children killed in the harvesting harrows or themselves left homeless under the teeth of spring earth turning.

On Wednesday some people came up from a church called God Is Love. Their leader was a Brother Willard Mitchell. I don't know how they found out about what was happening to us—the Angelus prayers and Mama's table grace and what Kelvin said we could do and what we couldn't—but he and the other brothers seemed to know about it all in detail and they told us they thought we were being treated unfairly and that it was un-American and against freedom of religion. They said we should take the case to court. They were so angry about the whole thing, it seemed all of a sudden to put a new light on what we had accepted so easily as Kelvin's law. They said it was an issue that was beyond just us and the Croom or even SCELP, but that it was "at the heart of" Americanism and civil liberties.

"Brother," Brother Willard said to Dad, "I hate to see the government making a sacrifice of you. You're a patient man; you've put up with a lot that I can see and we don't aim to mix in where we ain't wanted, but a man needs help sometimes to go against a government that's checking his freedom and taking away his independence."

Dad was confused and so was I. We didn't know what they wanted or how the members of the church thought they could help. While we were talking, Mama brought some lemonade out to the brothers. I could see they were impressed with her pioneer clothes. She did seem to be more comfortable in them now that she had gotten used to wearing them and wasn't kicking at them and fighting them from the inside. The brothers were very mannerly, taking the lemonade and saying "Thank you, ma'am." It warmed Mama up and she began to tell them the plans she had for the Fourth of July. "That's just the point," Brother Willard said, "we're patriots, too. We care about this blessed land and its rights." Mama gave him a big smile and said she agreed and why didn't he and these

177

brothers here come up and celebrate with us. She told him we were having some neighbors up, people from Bascom who felt the same way they did, patriotic. They could bring their picnics and there would be games and a hayride for the kids. The brothers said it sounded like a fine idea.

I was in town on Thursday for supplies. After the Fourth we would be having people almost all summer without interruption. I saw five or six people—Joel Bittner works at the Seven-Eleven, Tom Flowers at the hardware store, and some of the kids were just hanging out on the street. I invited four or five people to come to the picnic and bring their friends and families. Bobby Kinear looked at me funny when I told him. He said, "I heard you people went religious or something. Are you going to have prayers and speeches up there?" I asked him what had given him that idea, and he said he had heard it— that we had joined some new church and did special things because of it. I told him it wasn't so, and that we were no more religious than we had ever been, and that we weren't even allowed to say a table grace, except between visitors, now that we were on SCELP, but that we could ring the Angelus bell and stop if we didn't tell anybody why we were stopping. It was interesting to remember back to the times when nobody cared what we did or how we acted at all. Now, everybody knew or thought they knew all the details of our lives and actually had opinions about them. Bobby was saying he had heard things about our having religion. I told him again that it wasn't true. He said he was glad then, because he had always liked us, and he thought SCELP was a good idea, but that freedom of religion meant freedom from religion as far as he and his folks were concerned. I had forgotten that the Kinears were very strong atheists, but when he brought it up, I remembered that all through school he hadn't saluted the flag or said the pledge and the family

had made a big point out of not being in Christmas programs. I told him he was surely welcome at our place
and there wouldn't be any problem about his having to
pray. I saw Rudy Garner and told him. I told Andy Lock-
eridge and Mary Blascovic. I had gone out of my way to
go where Mary worked, even though our thing is over,
I guess. Mary didn't realize that a week of Dorothy Van
Houghton changes a man. Of course, Mary didn't know.
She was batting her eyes and moving around and doing
that smile-frown business that's supposed to keep men
guessing how she feels. Sure, she's pretty, but with all
those poses and plays she uses, I wondered how I ever
really thought she'd be interested in me. I told her about
the picnic. I was friendly, but no more. I told her that if
she had heard things about us going to church, it wasn't
true. Then I left. In the second I turned, I could feel her
surprise. I have changed so much because of Dorothy . . .

Mama went to Bascom, too, and when I saw her that
evening, she said people had come over and praised her
for the stand we were taking, while others said they
hoped the rumors and talk about us were mistaken. She
said, "Was it something I did or said and then forgot?"
I said I didn't think so. I told her people had the idea we
had gotten very religious. She laughed and said, "What
next?" After dinner we were sitting out on the porch and
Kate sighed and said out of nowhere, "I wish sometimes
I had the old days back—weren't we more peaceable then
in our minds?" Louise and I jumped on her, reminding
her of all the things we had now, benefits. The truth was
that we were all afraid to wonder things like that because
it was too late to go back. We jumped on her so hard she
got up and went inside. I feel sorry for her; she had no
dream hill to climb, no dream grove to lie in. I can work
hard all day and still have Dorothy, like a horizon, there
whenever I look up, even for a minute. Dorothy rims my
world. Still, there's work that needs to be done and I do

179

it and there's satisfaction in that. It's the idle times, the so-called rest times, when I don't rest at all but go back and back to Dorothy and our talks and the life I told her about—college, a time away to learn something besides what's here, even though I love it here. Everything suddenly seems useless and sad to me. It's a kind of hopelessness I guess old people feel; people as old as Dorothy.

17

Kate

Robert Luther was going around the place like Jane's drawing of a longhorn calf. And I was the only one who knew what the cause was. We had a third planting of hay to do and the home field to see to and the new people to plan for and now Mama's Fourth of July party. We made flags and decorated them. Jane drew about thirty pictures which we tacked up all around the fences and the big arena where people would park, and I made signs which we put out on the road and at the first and second logging trails to guide people in, and four other signs to tell them where to park their cars. Then we watched the weather report and hoped it wouldn't be too hot.

The Fourth was bright blue like a banner. We had cleared five acres of the home field, close-mowing so people could gather there without getting burrs or having too many insects. We carried the water barrels around near the trees and set them up on hay bales and figured with the room we had and maybe a hundred people, they could park on the north and follow the sun or shade around as the day went on. It was going to be pretty hot out there about noon.

When the Fourth came we were up so early and working so hard that there was no time to go and greet people. At the last minute we realized that the burlap bags we were putting out for trash wouldn't hold the wet stuff people were used to dumping along with everything else. Plastic had made that possible and we didn't have any—we worried about that for a while, and dippers for the water, and all kinds of details here and there. Robert Luther harnessed Achsa and Nebby to the pull bar of the hay wagon and tried the new rig out, and then we had to unharness and get the hay down for the hayride and fill the wagon and then rehitch, and by that time we were so hot and sweaty we all had to take bucket showers in back of the house.

It was noon before I had time to look at the way people were using the space in the field. Then I noticed an odd thing. The cars were not where we thought they would be easiest to park. The picnickers had parked in two different places; one group of them was on the north and one on the south—sunny, hot, and inconvenient. The picnickers were also in two groups, one at the northeast edge of the field and one at the southwest. It seemed strange to me why they shouldn't all want to go over to one side, but I was busy and didn't do any more than look and then go back for the other wagon where we had more water.

By noon we could see there were already more than the hundred or so people we had planned for. Every time Louise went out to check, she came back with reports that the count had gone up. At first Mama was happy about it. Louise was telling us all the people who had come—Robert Luther's school friends and mine and people we knew. We planned to go out later when the work was done and visit with them. Mama had invited Mr. Kelvin and his wife and new baby to come up and have lunch with us at the house. They came before noon, and we admired the new baby and ate, and then sent Louise to the field again to see how things were going. She came back and said there were lots more people than we had planned to have, and that they were setting up in an odd way in the field. When Mr. Kelvin was talking to Mama, Louise whispered to me, "Kate, I never saw any of those people in my life and they're not from Bascom, either." Louise exaggerates. I nodded, and Mrs. Kelvin asked me to give her a tour of the barn. When we got back, it was one-thirty, and I went out to the field to check the water barrels and see what Louise had been talking about. I was amazed.

The two groups had gathered at each end of the cleared area and were crowded together in a tight mass, leaving a bare space up the middle from the road to the unmown acreage about sixty feet wide. As I looked closer, I noticed the groups were different and that they were both acting differently from the way I had imagined the picnickers would. They were quieter, for one thing. There was some friendly talking, and now and then bursts of laughter, spottily from parts of one group or the other, but it was polite, as though people were indoors in the house of a stranger, and there was no joking and laughing *between* the groups, no feeling of holiday, and the way they were standing—they seemed—Daddy would say, "took up." I tried to study it a little. It seemed as though the groups were facing out, away from each other, and their talk, if they looked at one another, was a buzz, half whispered, and reminded me of hot August in long grass. I noticed that on the north, the cars were bigger and the people on that side were dressed better; their clothes were brighter and cleaner and at a distance they looked richer. On the south, the cars were smaller and dirtier and the people looked sloppier and poorer. I thought that for some crazy reason the picnic had divided itself into rich and poor, and then I came closer and saw that this wasn't so. On the north, the cars were clean but they were older, Chevies and Fords or pickup trucks. On some bumpers were stickers: GOD AND COUNTRY; PRAYER—EVERY CHILD'S RIGHT; HONK IF YOU LOVE JESUS; SUPPORT YOUR PRESIDENT; PROTECT THE FIRST AMENDMENT. Many of them had flags on the bumpers of their cars and gun racks on the insides. On the south, though the cars were dirtier, they were more expensive and they were mostly foreign. Instead of gun racks, they had ski racks, and their bumper stickers said GREENPEACE and NUCLEAR FREEZE and PROTECT THE FIRST AMENDMENT. I stood all alone in the empty strip between them in my long calico dress. I was wearing my sunbonnet and button shoes. I tried to think of something I could say to everybody, but even if I had wanted to yell across at them there were too many and the sounds of the day and the distance would swallow my voice. Besides, I didn't know what I could say to all those people that would remind them that this was a day supposed to be put aside for having fun—that it was America's birthday party. Then I thought maybe if everyone ate and drank and felt pretty good, maybe they would just get on with the picnic and then go home. I wanted to run back and tell Robert Luther about what I had seen, but I thought if I ran, something bad might happen, so I smiled and waved to both groups and they smiled and waved at me, standing there alone sometime between 1880 and 1889 and shaking a little, if anybody was close enough to see. I turned after a while and walked as slowly as I could back to the house, and seeing the Kelvins there and Mama and Daddy busy with them, I left there and ran for the barn and Robert Luther. I found him and told him what was happening down at the home field.

He was adapting the horse rigging for the hayride. "It can't be as bad as all that. Maybe that open space is an advantage." He was doing to me what I had done to Louise. He was saying, "That way I can take the wagon straight down the middle and then kids from both sides will get on and when the grown-ups see that—"

"You're not listening," I said. "I heard some firecrackers popping here and there—just little ones, but it made me think."

"About what."

"About these being city—well, town people, and that town people, even though their folks might have been country-born, have forgotten a lot of things."

"Like what."

I knew I had his attention then, because Robert Luther is very smart when he isn't "taken up." "Firecrackers, anger, and straw," I said.

He stood still and listened to me. He had been working hard and there was a dark line across his forehead where his hat had left dye loosened in his sweating. There were streaks of sweat on his face, too, and bits of straw clinging there like the yellow pollen we get in June. He said, "You're serious about this, aren't you—about this danger."

"Come and look."

"Where's the family?"

"They're up entertaining the Kelvins and getting the flags and streamers ready to put on the wagon."

"Dad went over asleep by the chicken coop before, so we don't have to worry about it."

"I think you need to come and see this; I really do."

He sighed. "Suppose you tell me."

"Have you seen the people over there?"

"I went out earlier this morning to take a look. There seems to be quite a lot of people."

"Please come down with me." I pulled him by the

hand and we went out of the barn and catty-corner over an edge of the second field down a little falloff to the home field.

I saw Robert Luther's eyes go wide. "Where did all these people come from? Who are they?"

"That's what I've been trying to tell you."

While I was gone, some signs had come out, sprouting on either side of the open swath: KEEP GOD IN THE SCHOOLS . . . ; FREEDOM FROM RELIGION . . . ; MY GOD AND MY COUNTRY . . . ; KEEP UNCLE SAM OUT OF MY CHURCH. There weren't many, but some people had planted them in the little ridges of earth left by the harrows and some had tied them to the trucks and cars. We understood then at the same time what had happened. We saw it suddenly and we saw it whole and we saw it too late.

There was a dust-up along the road and we turned at the sound of a motor behind us and saw a panel truck, white with blue letters: KOA-TV and the big number 4 with the circle around it and the four rays coming out of it like the sun. We watched it stupidly as it went past us up the road and then stopped at the barn and turned right. Robert Luther jumped suddenly and said "TV" in my ear, and began to run for the truck, which had turned and was coming down the middle swath between the two groups. I began to run, too. I couldn't keep up with Robert Luther and I wasn't sure what he had realized so suddenly until I was almost there.

TV. I put the two ideas together. It was what both groups had been expecting, wanting, needing, without quite knowing it, and the TV people . . . I thought suddenly that if a fight did break out, it would make a better story for them than if no fight broke out. This was not to say . . . I didn't think these things so much as feel them while I ran, that just the truck with its sign was a signal that we had to see in a certain way; I thought it meant we were supposed to act the way people act on TV—that

186

TV reports wars and because TV was reporting us, we were in a kind of . . .

It was true. There was a long minute when everyone was just as still as Angelus, watching the truck go by, and then they went into a boil behind it, waving their signs and yelling, and someone—a kid, probably—threw some part of his uneaten lunch; I saw pieces of something flying up and then there were more fruit peels and chicken bones. Robert Luther had stopped dead and was looking one way and another, trying to think what to do. He was on the edge of the fight, and now and then he was hit by food gone wrong, but nobody was aiming at us. There was a lot of screaming as people tried to get away, and some people who had been hit by things and were scared. I caught up to Robert Luther and we both realized another thing at the same time.

The TV and the riot were modern and we weren't—the Croom wasn't. The TV depends on modern help: police and paramedics and helicopters with bullhorn voices telling the crowds to disperse. None of that would happen here. We had no phone, and even if Robert Luther went for police, it would take three-quarters of an hour for them to get here even with TV help. Rioters are safe, in a way, in city hands, in modern hands, law and medicine three minutes away. It may be what makes them free to go as crazy as they do. Robert Luther yelled at me above the noise of it all, coming closer, "I have to get to the truck. I have to tell them there's no one to stop this. They may have a loudspeaker."

I yelled back, "It's dangerous."

"I have to do it. What if somebody shoots?"

Robert Luther had a purpose and the rioters didn't. He bent low like a football player and broke into the mass of people. I saw him go ten feet, fifteen, and then the bodies closed around him and he was hidden. If only he had told me what to do. If only I could think of something

187

myself, some way to get the crowd's attention, to tell them—what? I saw that they were beyond knowing, or beneath it. I kept looking at the gun racks in the truck windows. I couldn't look away. Not too many people could get to their trucks or cars, but if one did, he might—what if someone fired shots over people's heads and that got them to think and be scared and stop? What if they heard the shots and only thought someone was shooting and that they had better start shooting, too? I stood on the edge of the tangle and the sound of screaming and cursing and looked around for something to do. Where was Robert Luther? Why hadn't he come on the loud-speaker yet? Maybe two minutes had gone by, and maybe twenty, since he had gone into the mess. I looked back at the house, knowing they couldn't see us from there; we were too far and too far to hear, either. There is the smallest dip in the land that hides the bottom of this field from the house. There Mama and the girls would be serving tea and punch and cookies to Mr. Kelvin and his cute wife, and it was July 4, 1880. One Eye was probably up at the new shebang with charcoal, which he said he would bring this week as a supply when we started the new brewing. July Fourth was a big day for those veterans, but something told me One Eye would not be with them. Maybe he was drunk up there. My mind went from one thing to another, looking, picking, touching now this idea and now that. I had stopped thinking straight.

It was because of this that my attention was not on the world, I mean the world outside my mind. I began to have a feeling. The feeling was a kind of humming in the ground, a vague, remembered thing. I thought of a flash flood we were in, Robert Luther and I, when I was ten, when the almost dry river suddenly broke open and water high as a house came rushing down on us. There had been a throb a moment before. I thought it was the people jumping and screaming because the throb was

188

not a sound I remembered well. But it was coming from the ground. Where had I felt it? When had it been?

The memory came too late. Only something at the far side of my eye, where sight tells lies, made me turn and remember. The green wheat in the upland field was moving in a broadside line wide as two houses, and for a moment I thought it was Daddy harvesting at this odd time, showing Mr. Kelvin some pioneer thing. The wheat was green still and not ready to be taken. Then I saw the horns above it and they were the mowing. I couldn't believe, I couldn't take in the truth of it. All my mind would say over and over was: the gates. Someone left the gates open and Daddy will be angry. Did we ever tell One Eye, since we moved the shebang across the road about the two gates he had to . . . While they came down and down on us, mowing, mowing.

A stampeding herd stays together. The longhorns blasted by between me and the crowd so neatly that when they were gone, none of my clothes was ruffled and there was an even layer of whitish-brown dust all over me from the wind of their passing.

South of us the land slopes down again and goes to rock and forest. The herd would stop or go over a bank and break legs on the rocks. I had stood still as they beat on past me. There was a huge, blinding dust-up, a sudden . . . *climate* they made as they went past; the air was brown and thick and couldn't be breathed. There was a hot wind, but with it all the air seemed to have been sucked away. With the pound of their feet—not a rhythm like horses—no other sound was loud enough but directions, even up and down, were lost and time and distance had no meaning. It was over in a minute, yet it seemed to have gone on forever. Now I was looking at the hole they had made. Everything was completely quiet; food, clothing, bodies littered the ground. A further clearing and I could see people had drawn away back and they all hung in shock, totally still. The white-brown dust settled, but the air was misted with fine, shining particles on the other side of the corridor the longhorns had made. It seemed like a long, long time. Then one of the "dead" bodies and then another turned on the ground and rolled up on an elbow and then sat, feeling for broken bones. From somewhere a woman yelled. A baby cried. Then people began to scream and cry out; dogs barked from their tethers. The "dead," all the same brown color, like statues, rose up one by one.

In the beginning, there was laughter and gratitude because no one had been killed. There were two broken wrists and maybe broken ribs and "shock" and lots of bruises, and we turned into a first-aid station all the rest of the day, while one by one the picnickers, believers and nonbelievers all mixed together, limped away down the road for home. Mr. Kelvin collapsed. He cried first and then he went running here and there, as though he were trying to believe what had happened. Mrs. Kelvin put the baby down and told Jane to watch it in its little carrier and tell her when it cried. And then she became an administrator, a good one, telling me to take names, and she checked everyone out for injuries and got families organized and had Robert Luther check again as the cars left and had Mama serve water and coffee to people, while she did the bandaging we needed and told anyone who had been hurt or felt shaken to go to the doctor when they got down to Bascom.

It wasn't the longhorns who had overturned the TV truck; we found that out later. It was people mobbing to get away from the stampede. More of them were injured by one another than by the longhorns. Cattle know where they put their feet; they have to. People are not as delicate as cattle and their weight is not as evenly distributed. We saw people who had the marks of single hooves on them, bruises almost like big fingerprints where the long-horns had ridden on them, skipping over with the lift for spring a runner would do over a fallen tree or a smooth stone. Hours later we rounded up the longhorns, who had bunched together at the southeast end of the home field and then gone back, skirting the woods to where there was still green wheat. We had to get them rounded up and back to the riverbank before they foundered. Some of the people seemed proud to have been in a stampede on the Fourth of July. They didn't think about suing us until the next day, after they had told the story around to their friends. Some were just grateful and said so and limped away, and the gun-rack people helped the ski-rack people and the Prayer In helped the No Prayer In and the Greenpeace people gave the No Freeze people aspirin and Valium for the way down.

After everyone had gone we went over the field, and the next day we plowed it under because it looked like a dump. Some of Jane's calves were dead in the middle of it. Daddy said their hearts had probably given out in the run. He was surprised that they had gone the distance, he said, "All the way from the high pasture on guts and gristle," because they were still young—still nursing. Jane cried and Robert Luther took her out on the porch. They sat on the top step and I could hear her high voice and his deep one back and forth for a while. It was the usual stuff you tell a kid and it made me sad because I suddenly felt too old for what he was saying, almost as though it were a fairy tale. Yet, what he said was true.

There are all kinds of lawsuits against us. We are still getting names of people who are suing us for back problems and headaches and psychological shock. There are lawsuits from eight people whose names are not on either of our lists, Robert Luther's or mine, not the hurt list, not the unhurt list, and who I don't think were even here. Four government agencies besides SCELP are down

191

on us for things they think we did, while we tried to live in the 1880s. The agriculture people saw the longhorns and praised them to the skies, and then slapped a fine on Daddy and a quarantine on them because they hadn't been inspected or vaccinated or any of the rest of it. Forestry, Parks, Department of the Interior. Fines, imprisonment, or both.

The man from the bank laughed at us. The man from the Internal Revenue Service laughed when Daddy told him we were working backward into time. He said there was no IRS in 1886 and then he told Daddy we might go to prison because we hadn't filed on all our income in kind, being on SCELP as we were.

But we had gone back; we had been as clever and strong as those real pioneers. We had made it through summer and winter and hard visitors, and we had showed Bascom we could be more and do more than it ever thought we could.

I don't know how the upper pasture gates got open or how the longhorns got stampeded. I know that once they were going, the open way led right down into this field. Robert Luther says it was One Eye, wanting to ruin SCELP for us, seeing the longhorns and knowing about the picnic and starting the longhorns down to where the people were. What happened wasn't our fault; we were glad no one was badly hurt. None of us knew most of those people who came up for the picnic. We told that to the sheriff's men and the state's attorney's men and the federal marshals who came later. We did advertise in the Bascom paper and we had put notices on the Bascom church bulletin boards, but there were only about thirty Bascom people and they said they didn't know the ones who came. None of that matters now. I told Mama that. She keeps adding it all up to try to find the answer to it, why it happened.

If I add it up, I get two numbers, or two scenes: one

bright and sunny and one dark and awful. To the bright days I add the times I saw Mama smiling on the streets of Bascom, greeting people and having them greet her, and the smile she smiled then, and how she climbed back in the truck once and winked at me and cried out to Robert Luther, "Lovely day, lovely day." I add the bright and dark of being aware. Our artificial pioneering made us too self-conscious. We watched people watching us. Because of that watching, we lost the naturalness of the way we moved and talked to one another. All of us except Mama. She never changed except to get happier when people were nice to her, but people were able to accept her in 1880 better than they seem to now. Bascom is back the way it was; I'm still not sure why. Daddy changed some. I guess it was us, the kids, wanting SCELP to work so much, who did most of the changing, trying to be something we weren't—no, something we really were but didn't know how to be.

For Mama the total comes out with the bright days winning. For Robert Luther, the sum is a number I don't yet know—Dorothy Van Houghton, whose hair was dyed and who was old, really, but who gave him a way to that other world and took him through the door, smiling, to the place I'm afraid of. I want my body all to myself. I want to be the only one *here*, but I have feelings now, beginnings of long-lonesome feelings that have no names except for the songs we sing at school and they let us play on the jukebox in the cafeteria.

Not everything for Robert Luther was bright days. Mr. Kelvin was always at him for the money he spent on his hats. He had to ask for money all the time, and he and Daddy had to put every judgment to those invisible outsiders. It makes me angry in a way I never knew you could be, and they had that the hardest of all of us because they're men and not used to it.

There are going to be people from the Agriculture

Department here for months checking everything. Land people. Lawyers. The IRS, the county attorney's office. The Department of the Interior. Wildlife. Parks. And, of course, all of Mr. Kelvin's bosses in SCELP. People think we may lose the ranch. Others say no. Some people say we have embarrassed the government. I think the government has embarrassed us.

The funniest thing is that what we did most against the law, the popscull, wasn't what got us into trouble. No one knows about that to this day, and we are still paying for our food by running product to One Eye's men's club, although since we have to be so careful, Daddy went back to his old amount. He did triple the price, though. Robert Luther told me how that happened.

The Teeters and the Kirkseys were from Kansas, and while they were here they talked about Kansas being a dry state. We have a guest book—Mama's idea to remember our visitors at Christmas. On a hunch, Daddy got Robert Luther to write to both of them and ask what their product prices were. Mr. Kirksey wrote back about what he paid for his "unlabeled goods," and Robert Luther was so surprised, he went down to Bascom and called and asked Mr. Kirksey twice if he meant per quart.

So I add sophistication, which is what you get by knowing people from different places and thinking about it a little. One Eye bucked and kicked and showed his burned side and all but set fire to the rest of his face, but Daddy knew the right price then and we set the visit well away from his sleeps. The longhorns were no secret anymore. One Eye had to take the news, and after a fight, he came around.

Sophistication. It's bright and dark, both. Jane will be in second grade this fall and she won't go there as dumb-loving as she used to be. She fell in love last year with Mr. Kelvin and then she fell out of love. She tried to love all the visitors and she drew all their pictures, and she got to see some of them lose those pictures or throw them away or use them to wrap glass bottles in when they were packing to go. That's hard at any age, but harder when you are six, if I remember right. She found out she couldn't love everyone and that some people would not love her no matter how sweet and pretty she is. She saw the calves she loved die, and that made her know that what she loved had a will of its own and reasons of its own, too. It's knowledge I need and don't want to be given and don't want to face with Robert Luther and that Dorothy he aches for. I see his face sometimes when he doesn't think anyone is looking.

Louise came off best in this. She's writing it all down in poetry. They learned haiku in school last year and she has decided to write a whole series about all the visitors and another about how the land changed. She has already written a poem about the stampede, which she didn't see until it was over. In the poem we left the home field unplanted for a year and it sprouted plastic. We weeded the plastic wrap and harvested plastic flowers and freezer boxes. The poem made Mama laugh and Daddy said, "This child is gone crazy workin' for the government."

A brightness I should add is other people's vision of the Croom. I said before that the visitors made us self-conscious in our talk and thoughts; that we posed. I'll admit I did, a little, and so did Robert Luther, wearing his hats. But those same people saw our mountains, our trees, our sky in ways we had been too busy or too unsophisticated to see. We love this place, all of us, and while Robert Luther is hoping to leave, to go away to college someday, and I would like to go, also, I want to come back, even though I may have changed again. The visitors showed us what we have, how the fences curve with the hill, how the barn's lines fit with the hill behind it, as though the hill were holding it close.

195

Mama has started collecting pictures to repaper the parlor wall. They don't have to be 1880 now, but her tastes have changed in this past year. She says she'll keep bands of black and white between the pictures of people she wants to admire. It's more tasteful, she says.

Some of the people in Bascom took sides—some said it was our fault, some defended us. It broke down the way it always had, between the people who liked us and those who didn't, between those who thought Daddy and Mama were shiftless and those who thought they were just unlucky.

Mama's only idea was to do what the rest of us wanted and to save the ranch. She says she will never go into town again. For all the years I can remember, people laughed at her because she is so wide open she'll tell you the dream she had last night and what she wishes she was eating instead of what's really there. I used to watch people shrug and laugh. I never really admitted how hurt and angry it made me and how it also made me a little ashamed sometimes, of Mama and Daddy. That was my secret. Louise made me see that the way I keep my secrets closes out the people I love and makes me feel superior to them, and when I think I am most wonderful, I am least wonderful. It was a hard truth to get, and a hard one to keep. It was what saved my friendship with town people. When we got on SCELP, I was happy about how we were celebrities and whatever we said was funny or brilliant or original and people wanted to hear Mama go on about making corn bread in a woodstove oven. Now it's back the way it was, only tender on all those places that got soft in the year we had our neighbors smiling at us. I used to be an exception to the family; now I don't think I am.

And we know the name for Daddy's sleeps; Robert Luther wrote it down: narcolepsy. Dr. Van Houghton wanted to study Daddy while he was asleep. He told

Robert Luther the government would give Daddy money for having narcolepsy, a handicapped grant, because having the sleeps keeps Daddy from getting a job. Maybe Daddy can tell one part of the government to take money from the other part, the handicap people whose money Daddy never put in for.

Dr. Van Houghton's putting a name to the sleeps has made them more dignified to all of us. It's like belonging in a certain special group. It would have helped when Daddy was a boy to tell people that name, and would have spared him lots of whippings and being laughed at. Now he says it's too late for the fame of it, but I think it helps him to know that special rare people all over the world have it, too. He even mentioned it a few days ago, the first time I ever heard him do that. It was in a way that let us know he was beginning to forgive himself for all the years of going over on a hay bale or sliding off his chair onto the floor. Robert Luther went to the library and looked it up and found out that Daddy's kind, the kind that is very regular and strictly timed, is especially rare—even in so rare a condition, and when Robert Luther told him that, he smiled and said, "Well, well, maybe we should send Van Houghton a postcard and say on it, 'The answer's still no, but it's the clockwork variety; every seven hours and no longer than fifteen minutes.'" Yesterday, before he slid off his chair he said, "Well, here I go."

The summer work is turning and we're into cutting and baling and the hard field work to feed our animals. We got the Angelus, thanks to Louise and Mama, and we're keeping that no matter how busy we get. At that bell, I stop and stand still for five minutes and look at the hurting blue of our tremendous sky piled in the west with clouds, which happens every afternoon during this season. I watch the undersides played with lightning.

I smell the hot sun on the pine needles if I'm up in the high pasture, and I hear the hawks crying and the sounds of the hill all around me. I smell the earth, the sage, the hot wind and the cooling shadows. Always before, the smells of things were what I noticed for danger: food burning or a gas leak in an engine or butter that has gone off or something Mama forgot rotting in the refrigerator. The visitors and the Angelus made me smell every good smell the Croom has and see every good sight, and I want to keep that, because it might help, that smelling, that looking, hearing, touching, while the lawyers and the Ag. men and the people who are going to decide what happens to us say their words and write their judgments. Daddy and the people who laugh at us in Bascom won't need to worry about me carrying a rain-soaked lilac branch into the courtroom the way Mama might, or scattering dried sage in the judge's chambers, or bringing laughter into whatever dry and laughterless rooms they call us; but in the dusty rooms of all those proceedings, in the drone of the law, I might, for a minute or two, move for the Croom like a riding hawk or walk the green wheat or hear our pines over on the northern hill brush the wind from the face of the moon.